DRAGON KIN

Sapphire & Lotus

SHAE GEARY

AUDREY FAYE

COPYRIGHT

Copyright © 2016 by Shae Geary, Audrey Faye

Prologue

Even a hollow victory was better than defeat.

Lovissa turned her back on the roar and din of dragons rejoicing in the valley below and headed into the dim dark of her cave, seeking comfort — it had been a long, hard battle. The elves were getting dauntingly aggressive, and far more organized. If the fiercely independent elf clans ever truly bowed their heads to one leader, Dragonveld would fall, as surely as night would come.

Leadership was the only advantage dragonkind had left.

She listened as a roar mightier than the others nearly shook the sky. Baraken, telling the tale of his bravery and might. He had displayed both magnificently today, a warrior in his prime, defending his homeland, just as it should be.

Unfortunately, they weren't the only ones who claimed the plains and caves of the Veld as home. And while one elf might be puny and no more bothersome than a biting insect, enough of them could take down even the most ferocious dragon. They had hurt far too many today in their hailstorm of arrows and magic.

Lovissa reached the back room of her cave, pausing a moment to soak in the stillness. The smell of roasted meat hung in the air, and strawberries. She had a particular weakness for the sweet red fruits, and the young dragons charged with her care and feeding took pleasure in providing them. Or so she hoped – in her day, serving the queen had been a high honor.

So much had changed since she was a young dragonet.

She turned herself around, feeling her scales brush against the soft furs that lined her nest. Cushioning for her tired bones and sore muscles, which would have to be enough. There was nothing that could make a soft landing for the heaviness in her heart. They had lost two warriors today. Dancing, happy Eleret, and angry, vengeful Kynan.

Kynan had brought about his own doom, flying headfirst into the mouth of the elven attack. A suicide mission if ever she'd seen one. Lovissa had known it would come – he had lost his beloved in the battle of midwinter, and had waited only long enough to know where his sacrifice might matter most.

He had taken a lot of elves to the Summerworld with him.

Lovissa curled her tail up and let her head rest on its dusty scales. Here she could shed a tear, for Kynan and for too many who had come before him. And several more tears for bright Eleret, who had been a particular favorite. Young yet, for a warrior, and headstrong. In another time, she would have been a dragon bard, composing ballads of valor and honor and glory.

Instead, she had tried to live them. Tried to give the dragons one more year in the Veld. And perhaps she had succeeded. The passes would close soon, winter storms keeping the elves tucked away by their clan hearths until the snowmelt came.

It was enough to make even a dragon wish for eternal snow.

Lovissa closed her eyes in the dark warmth of her room. Eleret's cheeky, flamboyant death must not be in vain. It was time for the queen to ready herself. To do the one thing that only she could do. Tonight, on the eve of their biggest victory in a year, she must take steps to prevent their final defeat.

Because it was coming. She felt it in every one of her old and very cranky bones.

* * *

Lovissa landed on the stone ledge with a thunk that would have thoroughly embarrassed her in her warrior days. Now, as an aging queen, she could only be grateful she'd made the landing at all. She preened a little in the starlight, knowing not a soul was watching — not any that were still alive, anyhow.

Her eyes sought out the Dragon Star, hanging low tonight on the west horizon. Growing tired, just as she was.

She huffed a light flame out nostrils that were still puffing from the flight to get here, and scanned the sky one last time, making sure no over-eager babysitters had disobeyed her strict directive to stay home. The warriors knew better than to defy their queen, but some of the younglings had chicken bones for brains and more energy than they knew what to do with.

Hopefully, Baraken would keep them busy cleaning up the mess he'd made of the northern end of Dragonveld — a just penance for having lost his temper with the last of the fleeing elves. A dragon warrior could be fierce, but they should never be foolish. A few days with the younglings ought to remind him of that.

Just as this night would remind her that she was no longer young.

Lovissa turned slowly to face the sweeping expanse of rock behind her, and the mouth of the cave that was the most sacred place in all the Veld.

It was here that the ashes of their former queens rested.

Speaking the ashes was not a task undertaken lightly. Lovissa had come here only twice before in her reign, once to mix in the ashes of the newly departed queen, and once on a matter of sharp urgency and great loss.

As was this one.

She did not tarry on the ledge — the night grew cold, and the warm comforts of cave and kindred beckoned her old bones. She would come here for her final rest soon enough.

But not tonight. Tonight, she would ask the ashes what must be done so that Dragonveld would not be lost.

She walked slowly, regally, into the enormous cave, never taking her eyes off the shallow bowl in its very center. The bowl was enormous, the work of the finest dragon artisans. Formed from precious metals, encrusted with jewels and runes and the secret signs of kindred history, it would have enthralled most dragons with its otherworldly, eternal beauty.

Not Lovissa. She had eyes only for the plain gray ash gently mounded in the bowl's center.

Her head felt light and heavy at the same time. All the wisdom of all the queens, rendered by fire into its purest form. She bowed her head, the ridges of her nostrils mere inches from the bowl's edge. Hoping they found her question worthy.

Hoping they found her worthy.

She knew not to linger. Dragon queens had many virtues, but patience wasn't one of them. It was a foolish dragon who made a queen wait, even a dead one.

Gently, she blew fire onto the ashes, letting it run down the sides of the mound and curl back up the edges of the bowl. Runes lit and jewels sparkled, offering a silent dance as she formulated her question.

::Dragonveld is in danger. What must I do to make it safe?::

For a long moment, nothing happened, and Lovissa began to believe that she had come in vain.

Perhaps she was not worthy.

Perhaps her question had no answer.

Then the surface of the ashes rippled, and she slid back, feeling the light-and-heavy feeling in her head again. The queens would answer.

It took several moments longer, the top layer of ashes swirling like a dragonet chasing its tail.

And then the ashes began to rise, and in the dust, a dragon began to form.

Lovissa held her breath as the ashes shaped into the form, ghostly and beautiful, of Temar, the first dragon queen of memory. She was an enormous green dragon with glistening scales and claws as wide as they were long. A fierce warrior, and an even fiercer voice for peace and prosperity. Temar had established Dragonveld and begun the long journey of their kindred from nomadic beasts eking out lives on the edge of the world to what they were now.

Lovissa shivered under Temar's ghostly gaze. She did not want to be the queen who reigned over the end of days.

The ghostly shape of the oldest queen came to settle beside her. ::You have asked the wrong question, daughter. But we will answer the one you meant to ask.:: She held up a regal claw as Lovissa prepared to speak. ::Say nothing. Only watch.:: She turned and blew ghostly fire on the ashes.

It took Lovissa a long moment to realize the trembling she felt was inside her own skin. She took a long, deep breath and mimicked Temar's stern pose.

They watched together as the next queens rose. Elegant Citrin, and then tiny Alfalia — the smallest queen ever, and one of the most fondly remembered. Then came the pearly scales of Oberon, and Timosa with her kind eyes and spiky, ridged tail.

Lovissa named the dragon queens in her mind as they formed from the ashes, honoring each who had come before her, searching their gazes for wisdom she might take with her when she left.

Her eyes blurred as rosy scales formed, the ashes shaping into the glorious wings and sharp nasal ridges of the queen whose death had begun Lovissa's reign. She imagined she saw empathy in those eyes, and Arisen's typical lack of patience for anything that didn't involve fighting, hunting, or convincing one of her subjects to part with some of their treasure.

Arisen had been a renowned warrior, and an even more renowned coveter of shiny things. It had taken Lovissa most of a year to empty the queen's caves enough so that she could properly turn around in them.

Arisen's ghostly form came to sit at Lovissa's other shoulder. ::You must watch carefully daughter. Now, and as you return to cave and home. Do not see only the shiny things. The survival of dragonkind depends on the cunning of your eyes.::

That was a terrifying message from any queen, but this one in particular. Lovissa felt her insides trembling again, shaking her soul at its very foundations. Arisen leaned forward and flamed the ashes.

Lovissa tried to squelch the urge to scrunch her eyes shut like the tiniest dragonet.

She would watch, and she would know.

One heartbeat. Two. Five. A shivering breath and a moment of terror — and then the ashes began to form again. This time, Lovissa did not know the name of the queen with the ice-blue scales, or the story of her reign, or the lands over which she gazed. She knew only that she gazed on a queen to come.

Her heart began to beat again.

She would not be the last.

Deep blue eyes watched her silently – and then great wings spread, blocking half the stars in the sky. ::I will be called Fendellen. See with my eyes now. Dragonveld is in grave danger. But salvation comes, if dragonkind can be wise enough to see it, and be brave enough to embrace it.::

The ashes began to move again, fast, swirling shapes this time. And over the head of the ice-blue dragon queen, five shapes formed in the night sky.

Five dragons – and with them, riding on their backs, were five elves.

Fire hissed from Lovissa's nostrils. ::That cannot be.::

The ashes didn't waver.

Lovissa knew better than to challenge the collective wisdom of the dragon queens again, but every scale of her massive body resisted what she was seeing.

::Look clearly, daughter.::

She didn't have to look to see who had spoken. The reverberations inside her head made that clear. They all had. Every dragon queen speaking together with one message.

::The five will come. You must be ready.::

PART I:

It Has Begun

Chapter 1

Sisters were horrible, nasty creatures who should be taken to the edge of the world and thrown off.

Sapphire sighed. She already missed hers, all seven of them. Even if they'd teased her so much about her silly offering for the Moonwater Festival that she'd finally thrown all her precious possessions in a small rucksack and headed for the hills.

Or in this case, the forest, because apparently she'd managed to go the wrong direction, and there weren't any hills this way at all.

Which wasn't helping her already wounded self-esteem any. She was a reasonably competent elf, but when you were the youngest daughter of Moon Clan's ruling family, you were supposed to be special. Blindingly so, and every one of her seven sisters had been born with talents practically oozing out of them.

Then Sapphire had shown up, the strange child who loved the daytime hours and showed no signs at all of being remotely noticeable for anything other than her tendency to lose slippers practically before they'd made it onto her feet.

A boring elf in a family of bright moonbeams.

Which is why she'd had no idea what to make for her festival offering, and why she'd been sitting forlornly surrounded by small pebbles and feathers and flower petals and shiny things, wishing desperately for a moment of inspiration, when her sisters had landed. All seven of them, awash with their own brilliance and the added spark of Orion Featherdust's poem, which he had sent in an attempt to woo Adrial's attention.

If there was an elf under the age of forty who *wasn't* trying to woo Adrial, Sapphire didn't know who they were.

Which had just made her pathetic attempts to create a festival offering that someone might actually notice that much worse. Sapphire had fled to the sounds of tinkling laughter and the shame in her own heart.

This many hours later, she was finally willing to admit that she'd been at least as foolish as her fluttering sisters. There wasn't exactly anything noble in running for the hills with two days' worth of food, a pocket full of shiny pebbles, and no idea what you planned to do next.

She'd probably end up in one of Orion's poems. He had a sharp wit and an even sharper eye. And while he'd occasionally been kind enough to notice that Sapphire existed, she was pretty sure he'd happily trade in their limited goodwill for unlimited comedic potential.

The embarrassment would have no end.

Unless, of course, she managed to sulk her lost way into some actual trouble. The possibility of that was growing bigger by the minute.

Sapphire looked up at the moon and felt her hands tremble. It was very dark, very cold, and she wanted nothing more than to crawl into her soft bedroll of goose-feather down and pretend today had been a dream. But there was no point in wishing for things that weren't going to happen. Even her cousin Edric knew that, and he was only four. Moon Clan elves were realists underneath all their sparkle and shine, and she had inherited that much, even if she couldn't do anything worthy of a moonbeam. Her bedroll was far away, she had the poorest night vision of anyone in her clan, and even her bones were feeling the chill now. It was time to find a place to sleep.

She looked around, wishing she'd paid a lot more attention during Grandfather's woodcraft classes. He would know exactly how to sleep in the darkest of nights, safe and unafraid. Sadly, the only parts she remembered very well were the scary bits. If it looked like a cozy sleeping hollow, it probably was. For someone — or something — else. She shuddered. The last thing she wanted was to wake up face-to-face with a creature of the forest night.

She kept walking, turning her head at every sound. This far from home, the noises were all different. They sounded foreign to her ears, and a little sinister.

A twig snapped and she jumped sideways, and then had to scramble for her footing as twisty roots tangled around her feet.

Make that a *lot* sinister.

Sapphire exhaled, her breath harsh and loud even to her own ears. And then she felt a laugh slip from her lips. She wasn't actually a creature from one of Orion's poems, and she was probably scaring something else in the forest with her stumblings. She needed to stop creeping around like a scaredy-elf and figure out how to stay warm and dry for the night.

Squinting into the dark shadows, she looked for something that might be a trail, or at least a small clearing. The trees seemed a little less dense off to the left. Carefully, walking from one small patch of moonlight to the next, she made her way up a small rise and smiled. She could almost see her feet now.

Then something crunched underfoot, almost the same sound as when she'd stepped on her brother's kite. Sapphire winced and bent down to see what had broken. Under her soft leather moccasin was a sea-green shard, almost translucent in the moonlight. She stood up, cradling it in her hands, and held it up where the moon's rays were brightest. She'd taken care of the clan's chickens enough to know it was an egg shard, but it was like nothing she'd ever seen. Even in the weak, cool light of the moon, the piece of shell nearly glowed. The inside was smooth under her fingers, just like an oyster shell. The outside was gritty, almost like sand. Cracks ran through from where she'd stepped on it.

Sapphire didn't want to let the beautiful shard go. She crouched and looked around, seeking the rest of the shell and any sign of what might have hatched out of it. This was probably like Grandfather's tales of soft lairs and something she should be afraid of, but she simply couldn't find it in her heart to fear something this beautiful.

Snippets of some of Grandfather's more interesting lessons slid into her mind. The lore of the peoples of the world, and the creatures that shared their hills and forests. The ancient faeries and the newer humans. The tiny sprites and the glorious dragons.

Reverently, she touched her fingers again to the piece of eggshell in her hand. It glowed, just like she imagined a dragon scale might. No one of her clan had ever seen a dragon, but she remembered some of the stories. Wings as wide as a forest, eyes of fierce wisdom, breath of flame.

She couldn't remember any stories about how dragons were born, but eggs were as good a guess as anything else she could imagine.

She laid the glowing shell against her cheek and then looked up at the moon, grateful. Any forest that held something so breathtakingly lovely couldn't be all that scary.

Sapphire reached for her rucksack. She'd tuck the shell in with her meager food supplies and look for shelter. Perhaps now that she was less afraid, she might actually find something workable. She had the rucksack halfway open when what she'd seen high overhead finally registered. She frowned and squinted up at the branches again, sure her eyes were playing tricks, but they weren't. High in the winter branches, wedged in the crook of limb and trunk, was the oblong shape of what could only be an egg.

She stared at its faint glow, blinking. Dragons

most definitely did not live in the tops of trees — that much she would have remembered. And that egg looked like it could fall out any minute. She sighed — sometimes the clan chickens laid their eggs in some really silly places, but this set a new standard for ridiculous.

One that she felt compelled to do something about, but she had no idea what that might be. It would be a daunting climb in the daylight, even for the clan's best tree climber, and that very definitely wasn't her. But Trevan wasn't here, and she was — and whatever lived in that egg needed a rescue now, not whenever she could manage to find her way home and convince someone to help her.

Convincing Trevan would be especially hard. He didn't much like girls.

She looked down at the shell in her hand again, and the faint glow up in the tree that matched it — at least in her tired, fevered, homesick imagination. A glow that called to her. Tugged on something inside her that said this was the reason she'd run away, and it wasn't foolish at all.

Sapphire stared, and felt something inside her make a choice. The youngest, most ordinary daughter of the Silvermoon family had something she must do.

Moving slowly, she checked the ties on her rucksack and pushed her cloak back over her shoulders, out of the way of her arms and feet. The cold instantly made itself known, biting through the soft wool of her tunic and leggings. She grimaced and ignored her need to shiver. She couldn't very well climb wrapped in a cloak, however much that might seem like a good notion to her weary brain.

Her toes found purchase on the trunk, feeling their way through the moccasins and thick socks she wore. Fortunately, the tree was bumpy, with lots of protrusions to give her footholds.

Carefully, one slow movement at a time, she shifted a hand or a foot, seeking a secure hold just a little farther up the tree's trunk and inner branches. She remembered Trevan's words. Don't fight the tree — become one with it.

Grandfather had snorted and said the boy had the brains of a half-eaten leaf, but she wasn't going to think about that part. Or about the part where it had taken all the clan's healers four very long days to put Trevan's youngest brother's legs back together when a tree apparently hadn't liked his company.

She was just going to keep moving up in the moon-streaked dark, one very careful step at a time.

After what felt like an eternity of slow creeping upward, Sapphire paused, both feet on a branch wide enough to offer a less precarious perch than usual and her arms wrapped around the trunk that served as her only anchor in this high world, and looked up.

Her whole body was shivering now, and her fingers and toes no longer felt nearly as much as they had at the base of the tree. But hope rose because she was nearly there.

And fear — because from this vantage point, one thing was alarmingly clear. The egg was huge. Whatever was in there was much bigger than a chick.

Sapphire heard a whimper cross her frozen lips. She swayed into the exhaustion, the soul-stealing cold, the trauma of trying something she had no business doing.

And then heard that wordless voice, calling again. Heat rose from somewhere deep inside her, someplace fiery and warm that she hadn't even known existed. Determination. Ferocious intent, the kind that filled an elf girl of fourteen winters and firmed her backbone and had her moving her toes up the trunk again, seeking a way. Finding one.

When Sapphire's head crested the branch where the egg sat, she knew she could be the butt of her sisters' jokes and Orion's poems for the rest of eternity and it wouldn't matter. She'd made it. She stared at the pearlescent oyster shell and marveled. Its glow wasn't from the dim light of the reflected moon, but from something interior, right in the heart of whatever lived inside and readied to greet the world from such a precarious perch.

It wouldn't wait alone.

Her fingers moving more deftly, she carefully wrapped them around the egg that was bigger than her head and somehow managed to rearrange them both into the cleft where it had been. Her feet found another branch to hook around, her back found one to lean against, and with a little pulling and tugging, she got the heavy weight of her cloak wrapped around the both of them.

Hands full of exhausted reverence, Sapphire nestled the egg gently in the soft fabric of her tunic. It was winter wool and very warm, and it meant she could wrap one arm around the tree's trunk and hold on for dear life and her treasure would still be safe.

Which was a good thing, because that was all the strength she had left.

Her head leaned against the trunk, pillowed by the hood of her cloak. Sapphire felt her eyes closing, and smiled. Apparently, she'd found a place to sleep after all.

Chapter 2

So warm.

Sapphire could feel dreams floating her way, and hoped for a nice one full of hearth fires and warm blankets.

The egg in her lap agreed.

Her eyes flew open. Eggs didn't talk.

Apparently, they did get warm, however. Sapphire could feel the heat right through the arm of her tunic. She stared down into the recesses of her cloak. The egg glowed much more brightly now, in beautiful shades of pink and orange that reminded her of sunrises and the first peaches of spring. It was really warm — the parts of her touching the egg were quite comfortable, and even some of her a little farther away had almost managed to stop shivering.

The egg felt happy.

She blinked. This must be a dream. Eggs didn't talk, and they definitely didn't feel — she'd picked up enough chicken eggs over the years that if they did, she'd surely know it by now.

She shifted around and tried to get her other arm free. Words and feelings mattered a whole lot less than warmth right at this moment, and she could have kissed whatever magic was happening in her lap. Most little ones needed help to heat themselves, she knew that much from helping the healers stoke the birthing fires. This little one seemed to have the fire right inside its own egg, which seemed awfully smart, especially if its mother was foolish enough to lay it high in the reaches of a tree in winter.

She rubbed her hand gently over the pointy end of the egg. "I don't know who you are in there, but I'm thankful for the warmth you're sharing this night." It seemed wise to be polite — and she really was grateful.

The egg vibrated under her hand.

Sapphire gulped and carefully moved her fingers away.

The egg vibrated again, much harder this time.

She quickly grasped the egg with both hands. "Easy now, I didn't climb all the way up here just to end up dropping you because you got all wiggly."

Perhaps she was imagining things, but it seemed like the glow flickered a little, almost like it was listening.

The corners of her mouth turned up in a wry grin. She was lost, stuck in a tree, and talking to an egg. Orion was going to have a field day with his poem.

The light inside the shell shifted, looking almost like amused pink bubbles. Or Sapphire assumed they were amused, since the creature inside the egg clearly seemed to be.

This must be a dream.

She jolted as a dark spot rapped hard against the inside of the shell—and then stared, horrified, as a long crack ran lengthwise down the shell, splitting in two as it traveled under her hand.

"Oh, no. Not now. It's freezing cold out here and we're up in a tree and it can't possibly be time for you to hatch." Sapphire could hear herself babbling, but she was too tired and too panicked to do anything about it. The only thing that could possibly be worse than being lost and stuck in a tree would be to have some unidentified baby creature join her. Babies were hungry and loud and demanding and needed far more care than a warm and bubbly egg.

Another dark spot, another fierce tap, and then the egg grew another crack.

"This is a very bad idea." Sapphire used her sternest voice, the one that sometimes made her tiny cousins pay attention. "Just put your head back down and curl up all nice and warm and stay put in there, okay?"

The egg shook. Hard.

"How about I tell you a story?" Her brain couldn't come up with even the vaguest possibility of one. "Or I could sing you a song." She didn't have Arial's voice, but she could maybe manage a lullaby or two.

Her whole lap was vibrating now, and a lightshow danced just under the shell's cracked, crazed surface.

Sapphire took a deep, shaky breath. Whatever was in her egg was most definitely coming out. As carefully as she could, she wrapped her arms and legs and cloak into a nest. One with no holes big enough for a baby to slide through and fall to its death in a cold, dark forest.

A crack that sounded like a small earthquake, and then a fist pushed out through a small hole.

Or not a fist. Sapphire could feel her eyes getting wide. Those were most definitely claws. Long and purple and very sharp.

It suddenly occurred to her that even baby things could be dangerous.

She trembled and held fast. It wasn't like she had much choice — there was no way down and no way out.

The egg made another fierce cracking sound, and a head come out beside the purple-clawed fist. Two eyes looked straight at her, every color of green in the whole world in their depths. Vaguely, Sapphire noticed the pink coned nose, the shimmering peach scales, the spines running back from a broad, fierce forehead that were still covered in something glistening and wet.

None of those mattered. It was the green eyes, looking at her with all the trust in the universe, like she was goddess and clan mother and moon warrior all rolled up into one.

She could feel the answer rising up inside her, from somewhere way down deep. If she could be all that for this small dragon, she would be.

Sapphire had no idea how she knew that the creature she held was a dragon. She simply knew, just like she knew to gently peel off pieces of shell and wipe the wet, scaly face with the edge of her tunic. The baby dragon leaned into her touch, vibrating in a way that very much reminded Sapphire of her oldest sister's cat. "You like that, do you?" She grinned as a second claw emerged, and then what looked like shoulders, but instead turned out to be two pink, shivering wings.

Two really big wings.

She blinked as the rest of the baby dragon slithered out, a long scaly body and a spiny tail at least as long as Sapphire's arm. That was a lot of creature for one small egg, and it was all wings, tail, and spines.

And those two green eyes that never left her face.

Sapphire curled her head down, entirely enchanted, even as she kept wiping away wet slime with the corners of her tunic. "We have to clean you up so that you don't catch a chill in this winter wind." It sounded like the kind of thing one of the clan healers might say — if she was crazy enough to attend a birth high in a tree.

A long pink tongue reached out and started to help, occasionally rasping Sapphire's fingers as they cleaned. She grinned as the baby slurped a particularly long string of goo. "Don't tell me that tastes good."

All she got in reply was a rumble — and more slurping.

She shrugged, amused. Babies ate all kinds of weird things. She stopped wiping up the slime. If the baby thought it was food, she would just let it be. Her tunic was going to be hard enough to wash as it was, and her mother had firmly insisted, ever since they were old enough to hold needles and washing rocks, that all of her children were perfectly capable of restoring whatever damage they did to their clothing.

That held doubly true for damage caused by foolish walks in the woods.

She might get some sympathy for having a baby dragon born in her lap, though. Everyone knew births were *really* messy.

A scaly chin settled on her arm and green eyes looked up at her, blinking slowly. She could feel the huge, awed trust again — and something new.

Sapphire felt her heart grow right inside her chest. She reached out a gentle finger to stroke the peach-pink forehead. "I think someone's getting tired."

One blink and then another, each one a little slower than the last.

She held very still. No Moon Clan elf with any brains at all moved when a little one was on its way to dreamland, because her mother also had a rule about waking sleeping babies. Ever so slowly, green eyes made their way closed. One brand-new baby dragon, still half covered in slime and bits of shell, fast asleep. The most beautiful creature in all the world.

Sapphire laughed quietly as pink nostrils let out a whiffling snore. Definitely asleep.

She had no idea how they were going to hold tight in the tree all night, or how they were going to stay warm, or how they were going to get down in the morning. Part of her was scared out of her mind because this was far worse than running away from home or getting lost in a strange forest.

But the other part of her, the part with one arm wrapped around a strong tree trunk and the other wrapped around a tiny, snoring dragon, felt like something unbelievably important had just happened in her life, and no matter what happened in the morning, it could never be undone.

This small creature with the long tail and the sharp claws and the eyes that had been so full of trust — this creature needed her.

And that made Sapphire Silvermoon anything but ordinary.

She looked up at the deep night sky and the blanket of stars that nestled just over the treetops, and even though her teeth were only a hairsbreadth from chattering, she felt oddly content. She leaned her cheek against the tree and started counting stars. One down low on the horizon seemed to wink at her, and Sapphire laughed softly and winked back.

Maybe this really was all just a dream.

Chapter 3

Sapphire jerked awake, sure the demon hordes of hell were about to land on her doorstep and rend everyone in her clan limb from limb. And nearly fell out of the tree as she did so.

She screeched as her numb foot slipped off the tree branch, and somehow managed to juggle feet, tree, and baby dragon back into some semblance of order before they all plummeted to their deaths. Then she took a deep breath and tried to open her eyes again, because clearly she was still dreaming.

Teenage elves didn't wake up in trees with baby dragons on their laps. Especially not ones making such an outrageous, ear-splitting racket.

It took three tries before Sapphire convinced herself that her eyes were already open.

Memories flooded into her sleep-clouded brain of glowing shells and winking stars and the pure, innocent love of a shiny peach-pink baby dragon — one that bore passing resemblance to the small, shrieking monster in her lap. As well as she could with cold-numbed fingers, Sapphire tried to pat its head. "Hey, shh. You're okay, little one. We're safe up here." That last part wasn't exactly true, but in her experience, telling littles the whole truth wasn't a good way to get them to calm down.

The dragonet let loose another bellow, and this time, smoke came out its nose.

Sapphire could feel her eyes getting big. Her baby cousins sometimes had very fierce tempers, but none of them had ever set anything on fire.

She stared at the yowling creature in her lap and felt her whole body start to shake. Her muscles were so sore, she could barely move them. Her legs felt like two frozen blocks of ice, and she was up a huge tree in a strange forest with a tiny, fire-breathing monster.

This couldn't possibly be happening. She squeezed her eyes shut and tried to will herself back into a dream.

Something swooshed in the air right past her nose. Sapphire's eyes popped open, and she flinched, horrified, at the arrow embedded in the tree branch inches from her hand. Then she realized that the howling creature in her lap had gone totally silent, its eyes absolutely riveted on the small blue bag hanging down from the arrow's tip.

Moving as little as she possibly could, Sapphire's eyes cast around for the source of the arrow.

"Down here." The voice sounded far away and quite amused.

Very carefully, Sapphire tilted her head down toward the forest floor. Her head spun — it was insanely far away. She could make out the outlines of a woman who might be human or elf. She stared, wondering if she dared say anything.

"The bag's got some milk curds in it. If you can feed that to your youngling, that should hold her long enough for us to figure out how to get you down from there."

Sapphire had no idea how the stranger knew about the dragon in her lap, or that it was a girl, or what to feed it, but she was far too cold to look askance at such a gift from the heavens. With clumsy fingers, she undid the bit of rope holding the bag closed and offered a small bit of the lumpy white stuff she found inside to the very attentive baby in her lap. A scratchy pink tongue whipped out and slurped up the curds faster than a blink.

"Like those, do you?" Sapphire tried to take out another lump and gave up — her fingers were too swollen from the cold to do anything nearly so dexterous. As quickly as she could without letting go of dragon or tree, she poured the contents of the bag out onto a patch of her cloak. It would need the washing of its life if she ever got down from here, but at this very moment, that seemed like the least of her worries.

The baby dragon wrapped its tail tighter around Sapphire's arm and then made very quick work of the small mountain of lumpy white. It made a mewling sound in its throat as it ate — and almost immediately, its scaled belly started to warm.

Sapphire breathed out a sigh of gratitude and laid both of her hands on the sudden heater in her lap.

The dragonet squirmed, but didn't stop eating.

Sapphire giggled and tried to move her face closer to the heat too. "Sorry, I bet my hands are kind of cold."

"Do a good job warming your fingers up — I think you're going to need them to get down."

Sapphire's head snapped up. The voice was coming from far higher this time. She found herself staring again, this time at the person who had been on the ground moments ago and was now stretching toward them through the trees — on the head of a dragon the size of a small mountain.

40

Sapphire felt her entire body liquefy. A small, terrified screech slid out and she tried to bury her head under her cloak.

"This is Afran," said the voice calmly. "I'm sorry to frighten you, but we need to see if he and I can reach the two of you and help you out of your tree before this storm lands."

The tree Sapphire sat in swayed ominously, as if it agreed with the voice in the trees.

She scrunched deeper into her cloak. Whatever bravery she'd left home with had disappeared long ago. At this point, she only wanted to wake up and find herself in her bedroll by the fire with her sisters, all this gone as if it had only been a dream.

The tiny dragon in her lap started to make a chittering sound and licked her cheek.

Well, maybe she didn't want it *all* to go away.

"Hello, tiny girl." The voice sounded entirely unconcerned by the whole ridiculous situation. "You picked a foul morning to be born."

Sapphire peeked out of her cloak. "She hatched in the night."

The person with her legs wrapped around the enormous dragon's neck nodded, as if that made perfect sense. "They never do seem to choose times that are convenient. What chased you up the tree?"

Somehow that snapped Sapphire's backbone straight. "Nothing chased us. I saw the egg up here and came to see if I could get it down." That almost made it sound like she'd had a plan, except for the part where she'd never had any idea how she would get down again. She stared at the woman on the dragon's head, studying her face. It wasn't a young face, but not terribly old, either. It carried lines of fierceness and common sense and steadiness. Something in Sapphire relaxed. "Are you a warrior?"

The woman's head nodded slightly. "Of a sort. I'm dragon kin."

Grandfather's lore had covered that. The mysterious, mythical elves who lived with dragons and bonded with them. Sapphire swallowed hard. "Then you know where we need to take this baby dragon." Somehow, that didn't feel as good as she thought it would, even though she desperately wanted the small creature in her lap to be safe.

"For now, we'll be taking both of you." The woman cast a concerned eye at the sky, and then leaned down, putting her ear almost to her dragon's head. "The trees are thick here, and we can't reach through far enough to get you." She grimaced. "Which is lovely protection for the hatching grounds, but today, it's not working in our favor. This is as close as we can get."

Sapphire looked at the long distance to the dragon's huge head and gulped. Then she looked up at the sky and gulped harder. Roiling gray clouds were amassing and moving their way quickly. She was elf enough to know exactly what that meant. A storm, and a big one.

Even as she thought it, the first large, cold drops hit her nose.

"We need to move quickly." The woman's voice was brusque now, with little of her former kindness. "I'd climb up and get you, but I don't think that tree is strong enough to take my weight without swaying the two of you right out of it. And this rain is about to make the climb down far harder. Are your hands warm enough yet to manage, child?"

She wasn't a child, but even as Sapphire's mind protested, she knew that wasn't what really mattered. She was small and weak enough to pass for a child, and that was her true problem. "I don't know if I can." The climb up had been horrendous enough.

The dragonet in her lap let out a yowl.

The woman winced. "I'm also out of cheese curds. Sorry, little one." She looked Sapphire straight in the eyes. "I'm Karis, and I can see that you're tired and very worried about your small friend there."

She wondered what else Karis could see. "I'm Sapphire."

The tree swayed again, and her foot slipped on the branch. She grabbed at the trunk, trying not to whimper, and felt terror strike the little heart in her lap, too.

"Sapphire." Karis spoke in the kind of tone that said she expected to be obeyed. Instantly. "I need you to stand up for me. Get yourself a good hold on that trunk and find your first foothold on the way down."

She didn't have enough hands. "But I'll drop her."

"You won't." The dragon warrior chuckled. "She's got four tough little legs with claws that know how to hold on and a tail I bet she's already got wrapped around your arm."

It was somehow comforting that the woman knew that. Gingerly, Sapphire moved her hands away from the dragonet. Four claws promptly latched themselves onto her tunic.

"Can you climb with her there?"

Sapphire felt the pounding heart racing right next to hers. "I hope so. I don't think I can move her."

"Good. Then you don't need to worry about

her falling." Karis's voice was back to brusque. "Time to show off the fancy climbing skills that got you up that tree."

She didn't have any — and the rain was coming harder now. Sapphire shuddered to think how much harder this was going to be if everything got wet.

Closing her eyes, she laid her hands one last time on the warm belly of the baby dragon clinging to her for dear life, and spoke words meant only for the tiny creature's ears. "I'm going to do my very best. You hold on tight and don't look down, okay? And when we get to the bottom, I'm going to find you some more of those curds and you can eat as many of them as you like."

The fear billowing out of the little one's body dimmed a little.

Sapphire pushed back her cloak and stood. Then she reached for two nearby branches, scrabbled her feet down the trunk for a good foothold, and tried not to think.

It took ten eternities, or fifteen, or twenty. She was vaguely aware of the warm heartbeat against her chest, and the soft words of encouragement from the voice behind her, and the icy rain beating down on every inch of her skin and cloak and hair.

But mostly, she thought about the next foothold. The next handhold. The next step closer to the ground.

When her questing foot touched down on soft earth, Sapphire simply crumpled into a heap of boneless elf remains.

Strong hands grabbed her shoulders moments later, pulling her up to sitting. "That was very well done, child. Very well done."

A flask met her lips, and Sapphire swallowed convulsively. She wrinkled her nose at the strong, bitter taste.

The warrior beside her chuckled. "Sorry — my morning tea isn't to everyone's liking."

"It tastes like shoe rot." Sapphire was astonished to find that the voice saying that was her own.

This time Karis's laugh was bold, loud, and full of relief. "So people say." She reached out a hand and pulled Sapphire to her feet. "We need to keep moving. I don't guess you want to camp out here in this cold, and if we rest for long, those legs of yours are going to realize what a hard job they just did and refuse to move anymore."

Sapphire was pretty sure that moment had long since come and gone. Her legs felt like jelly, and she wasn't at all sure standing was a wise idea.

Four claws clutched her tunic a little harder.

She wrapped her arms reflexively around the baby dragon and felt it relax.

Karis peeked into Sapphire's cloak. "She's beautiful."

"I wouldn't know." Sapphire could hear her voice quivering. "She's my first dragon."

Karis chuckled and scratched the top of the baby dragon's head. "Such an unusual color. Like the lotus flowers that grow by the Bay of a Thousand Waterfalls."

The creature clinging to Sapphire chirruped happily.

Karis laughed again. "You'd like Lotus for a name, would you?"

Lotus. Sapphire had no idea what the flower looked like, or where a thousand waterfalls were, or how Karis knew what the baby dragon was saying, but it was a beautiful name—something that sounded like it came out of one of Orion's poems.

"This way, child." Somehow Karis had the three of them walking. "How did you end up here?"

Sapphire's brain didn't feel capable of conversation, but she tried. "I got lost. I do that a lot."

"Hmm." Karis cast a pensive glance back at

the tree they'd come down from. "No one finds this forest unless they're meant to be here, but that's something we can consider when we're fed and dry and sitting by a crackling fire."

Sapphire had never heard anything that sounded quite so good. Fierce tremors still ran through her body, even though she could feel and see her feet finally back on solid ground.

"We'll also need to send word back to your family, youngling. Which clan do you hail from?"

The one that was going to be ready to crack her head against a hard rock for being so foolish — and she was going to agree with them. "Moon Clan, over in the Early Waters Vale." Wherever that was from here.

"Ah." The warrior woman looked like she was thinking. "I don't believe we've had any of your clan arrive here before. Certainly not in recent memory."

If Grandfather hadn't included it in his lore classes, it probably hadn't happened.

"Come." Karis reached for Sapphire's rucksack and swung it easily over her own shoulder. "Can you carry the dragonet, or would you like me to?"

A tiny peach head emerged from the folds of Sapphire's cloak and hissed. It reminded her sharply that she wasn't the only one who had been terrified.

Karis touched a finger to Lotus's forehead ridges and grinned. "A spitfire, are you, little one?"

Sapphire shifted her hold. Her arms were exhausted, but clearly this was one baby dragon that wasn't going anywhere without a fight. "I can carry her."

The old warrior gave her a quick nod of respect, and then turned to the huge, hovering presence in the trees to their left. "Afran, when you get out of these infernal trees, fly ahead to the village and let them know to expect our arrival." She laid a hand on the shoulder of Sapphire's sodden cloak. "It will take us about an hour of walking—do you think you can manage?"

There didn't seem to be a whole lot of choices, and Lotus was already curling back up in the warm heat of the cloak, expecting the bigger, wiser creatures in her world to keep her safe. "I'll do what I need to do." She winced at the plaintive tone in her voice. "So long as there's a fire at the other end."

Karis laughed, loud and long and with the kind of appreciation that fed strength to Sapphire's legs. "There will be a fire, my girl, even if I have to get Afran to light it. I know Inga was putting bread in the ovens when I left this morning, so there should be some of that tucked away for us too, along with a bowl of her venison stew."

That sounded like Sapphire's idea of bliss. She extended her step a little, trying to find the ground-eating stride the older elves used when they had long distances to travel.

Karis chuckled and matched her, step for step.

Chapter 4

"We're here, youngling."

Sapphire tried to peel her eyes away from the sodden ground. She'd never been so wet in her entire life. Her wool cloak weighed more than she did, and her feet had stopped feeling like flesh and bones long ago. She managed to tip her chin up far enough to catch a brief rain-soaked view of where they'd arrived, and blinked at the first building she saw. It was curved, almost in the shape of an eyebrow, with walls running seamlessly into the roof.

"Come this way." Karis's arm tugged her off to the left. "The kitchen's just over yonder, and I'm sure Inga's got something to warm our bellies."

Food.

Sapphire found strength she didn't know she had left and followed in the older warrior's wake. Karis was saying things, pointing to things in the village that were probably important, but the words barely penetrated.

Then they stopped, and Sapphire realized they were inside a building. A dim one, and very small — but the rain had stopped. Not that it mattered much when she'd carried an ocean of it in with her. She could hear the drops running off her onto the hard floor.

Karis's hands lifted the sodden cloak from her shoulders. "Here. We'll get you down to clothes that aren't quite so wet, and then you can go sit by the fire and have a bowl of stew with Kellan here."

Sapphire blinked the rain off her eyelashes and realized there was someone else in the room with them. A younger girl with brown hair and lively, curious eyes, dressed in a simple tunic and leggings the color of new spring grass. The girl grinned and held out a cup. "I've got some mulled cider for you. Somehow the babies always seem to choose to come when it's wet or windy or cold."

"They're dragons," Karis said dryly. "They're not much bothered by the weather."

"That's fine, but the rest of us can't make fire in our bellies, so it seems like the babies could be a little more thoughtful." The girl settled the cider in

Sapphire's frozen fingers as she talked — and then giggled as a pink tongue dipped into the mug. "You've woken up, have you, little one? Cider's not for dragons. We'll send you with Karis and you can go have some nice milk curds."

Sapphire tried to juggle the mug and a suddenly very wiggly Lotus.

"Here." Karis held out her arm, palm down, like she was getting ready to land a hawk. "I'll take her over to the nursery and get her settled."

"No, I'll do it." Sapphire jumped, astonished she was the one who had spoken. "I want to stay with her."

"You need to get warm and dry and fed, youngling. You're no use to anyone if you catch your death of a cold, and Inga will hammer on my head for it too." Karis deftly moved Lotus to her arm as she talked. "I'll come back once she's settled."

Sapphire's heart was objecting fiercely, but her arms and legs could barely move, much less put up a fight, and Lotus didn't seem overly upset. She watched, bewildered, as the warrior left with a peach-pink dragonet wrapped around her arm.

"Come this way." It was Kellan tugging on her arm this time.

Sapphire followed the younger girl through a

narrow doorway and into a larger room — one full of heat and light and smells that could bring a hungry elf to her knees.

"It's venison stew with lots of mushrooms — Grady and I picked them fresh this morning."

Sapphire collapsed into a chair by the fire, ridiculously grateful to be off her feet. A bowl of stew landed on the small table beside her moments later. She stared into its depths, barely able to believe that something that smelled that good was real.

"Here, you can dip some of the bread in that. Easier than a spoon, and the bread's just out of the oven." Kellan broke off a small piece and held it out as if she were feeding a young child.

Sapphire was too weak and too hungry to protest. She dunked the bread in the thick, rich stew and nearly passed out when she shoveled it in her mouth. "Mmmmmppphh. Gddddth."

Kellan laughed. "I guess you like mushrooms, huh?"

She would have eaten every drop even if she hated them, but this was the best stew Sapphire had ever tasted. She managed to chew and swallow, and then picked up the cider to wash it down so she could start all over again. Even that was delicious, tasting of fall and cinnamon and apples so ripe they dripped juice everywhere when you bit into them.

She didn't bother trying to talk this time — she just sighed happily and took the next hunk of bread Kellan handed her.

She wondered if Lotus would like bread. Maybe she'd take her some once she'd finished. She took a small piece and laid it to the side of her bowl.

Kellan raised a questioning eyebrow.

Sapphire shuffled stew into her cheek to reply. "I was going to take it to Lotus when I was done."

Kellan grinned. "Dragons don't like bread — it gums up their fire. Irin and Kis will take good care of her now. They'll make sure she gets plenty to eat."

Sapphire felt curiosity rising up even through the stupor of the mushroom stew and the frustration that no one else seemed to think the baby dragon was hers. Kellan sounded like she knew things. "Who are Irin and Kis?"

"You saw the rondos when you came in, right? The buildings that look like really big cooking ovens?"

They'd been impossible to miss, even in the rain. "They looked warm."

"They are, especially with a dragon inside heating them up." Kellan handed over another chunk of thickly buttered bread. "The biggest rondo is the nursery, where the youngest dragons live. Irin and Kis take care of things over there. Lots of us help out sometimes, especially when someone's sick or teething, but they're the two in charge. They used to be fighters, but then Kis got a wing-wound and Irin brought him back here to get healed, but they still can't fly very well, so they stayed."

Sapphire tried to imagine a clan where the retired warriors raised the babies. "They sound scary."

Kellan nearly snorted cider out her nose. "Kis and Irin? Plenty, especially if you don't pay enough attention in weapons class or if you're silly enough to wake a sleeping dragonet. Irin threatened to cut off my head with his sharpest sword when I did that once. But mostly they're sweeties. They look fierce, but they'll take really good care of the baby you rescued."

She didn't want anyone else taking care of Lotus. "Maybe I can help."

Kellan looked skeptical. "Do you know anything about dragons?"

Just that they liked to eat milk curds and they had really sharp claws and the most beautiful green eyes in the world. "No, but I could learn."

Her new friend sopped up some stew juices with the end of the loaf of bread and popped it in her mouth. She chewed for a while, thinking. "We don't get a lot of new people here, but if you wandered into the forest, maybe you're meant to stay. I hope so. I bet you're a lot of fun when you're not soaking wet and tired."

It was nice to have someone think so. Sapphire spooned up the last of the stew in her own bowl.

"Ah, good — you're done." Karis's head popped around the corner, and then she walked into the room, still wearing her wet travel cloak and dirty boots.

Sapphire felt guilty that she was warm and dry and full. "I'm sorry — we ate all the stew."

"Of course you did." Karis laid a companionable hand on her shoulder. "Don't worry — I got a big bowl of it too. I've been over with Irin and Kis, helping Lotus get settled in."

A hundred questions bubbled to Sapphire's lips. She went with the fastest one. "Is she going to be all right?"

"Dragons are tough." Karis didn't seem at all worried. "She ate her body weight in milk curds and collapsed in a warm corner for a nap."

Kellan jumped to her feet. "I'll go tell Alonia we'll need more curds."

Karis's other hand landed on the serving girl's shoulder. "Already done. You can take Sapphire here and tuck her into a bed, as I'm guessing she could use sleep as much the baby dragon we just settled."

"She can bunk in with me. I've got lots of room with Lorett gone."

"Good." Karis seemed to approve of more than just the sleep arrangements. "Indira and Saven have gone off to tell Sapphire's clan that she'll be staying with us for a few days at least."

There was a long silence at that, one ripe with words unsaid and things that Sapphire didn't understand. But a whole night of sleeping in a tree had finally caught up with her, and she could feel herself swaying on the chair. She desperately wanted to go see Lotus, but she couldn't figure out how to stay awake another second.

Strong arms caught her as she fell.

Her last thoughts before sleep took her were of bright green eyes and peach-pink scales.

Chapter 5

This had definitely been the strangest two days of her life.

Sapphire rubbed the sleep from her eyes and wandered out of the small room where she'd woken up. Sunlight had streamed through the small window and teased her awake. There'd been a pitcher and basin of water and a chamber pot, all of which she'd made quick use of, but nothing else to tell her where she was or who had put her there.

"Ah, there you are. Good morning."

She turned to face the side of the room where the voice had come from. Karis sat at a small table, a pile of small metal parts spread out on a board in front of her. Judging by the big pile of dirty rags and the smaller pile of neatly folded ones, she was cleaning something.

Sapphire cleared her throat, a bit uncertain it would work. "Hello."

"We were going to put you in with Kellan, but you passed out on us and here was closer." The older woman gestured at a small counter. "There's fresh bread and cheese, or oatmeal if you'd rather, although it might be a bit cold by now."

Oatmeal was something she only ate if she was really sick. "Bread and cheese would be lovely, thank you. Do you mind if I toast it over your fire?" That was her favorite. Sapphire took a step toward the counter, and looked around, perplexed. The space was toasty and warm, but there wasn't a hearth anywhere in sight.

"The small rondos generally don't have fires. We mostly wander over to the kitchen for food." Karis gestured over her shoulder. "And Afran here is keeping us nice and warm."

Sapphire blinked at the surface she'd assumed was a wall, and noticed it was moving slowly in and out.

"There's no need for a fire with a dragon in the house." The older woman smiled. "I bet even the little dragonet kept you reasonably warm up in the tree."

They maybe had different definitions of warm. "Afran lives here? With you?"

"He does." Karis chuckled as a low rumbling sound filled the small room. "Fortunately, I don't mind his snoring."

Sapphire got a small plate of bread and cheese and a tumbler of something that smelled like the mulled cider of the night before, trying to be as quiet as she could. Afran's eyes had been kind in the early forest dawn, but he was huge. She didn't want to wake him.

Karis seemed to have no such compunctions. She reached for a small slice of the cheese. "Did you sleep well?" Her voice echoed off the walls, a woman used to being heard the first time.

"I did, thank you." Sapphire's well-schooled manners fought a battle with fast-rising curiosity, and lost. "What do you do here at the village? How do you get to live with a dragon?"

The woman cast a fond glance at the gently breathing wall. "We're teachers, of a sort. There's a school here, and we work with some of the students."

Kellan hadn't mentioned that part. Hope fluttered alive in Sapphire's chest. "How does someone become a student?" Maybe that would let her stay close to Lotus, at least. "Could I?"

"Well..." Karis looked undecided. "You made it through the Mirror, and that's no small thing. But you're also from an important elf family, and that's not typically who we take in."

Sapphire knew she wasn't very important, but that wasn't what caught her attention. "What's the Mirror?"

"It's a kind of magic. It keeps the dragon kin village hidden in plain sight, you might say. Very much like the Veils do for the elf vales." She smiled. "We're no more than a solid day's walk from your clan, but I bet you've never seen a dragon, right?"

A good night's sleep was making Sapphire's head work a whole lot better. "Never. And I didn't know about this village either, and I know people from elf clans that are much farther than a day away." Human villages in between the clans didn't tend to know much about elves because of the Veils. It made a strange kind of sense for the dragons to have similar protections.

"Exactly." Karis kept working on cleaning the metal bits of the tool she'd taken apart. "Dragons have tried living as part of the visible world, but they're easily misunderstood, and it tends to end in a lot of violence and hardship. We needed a place close to the clans to raise the young dragons and let them find their kin, and the Mirror helps protect us while we do that.'

Kin. That was a word from Grandfather's stories. A suddenly very important one. "Who gets to be kin?"

This time, Karis's eyes flickered with interest. "Some people, elves and humans both, form a special bond with a dragon. They become partners, and they spend their whole lives together."

Sapphire swallowed her bite of bread and cheese barely chewed. "Like you and Afran."

"Yes. We bonded shortly after my rising ceremony."

The official welcome of an elf to adulthood, and four long years away. "Is it always adults who bond with dragons?" Sapphire could hear the plaintive note in her voice.

"No. Usually, but not always. Irin and Kis bonded when Irin was still a child. And every year or two, one of our students bonds before their rising."

She needed to be one of those students. "Tell me about your school."

Karis's head tilted to the side. "We take in strays and orphans, mostly, and the occasional one who wanders through the Mirror with stars in their eyes. We offer an education at least as good as any in the vales, and a chance to make an important difference in the world when you're done."

Sapphire could barely breathe. "So I could stay. And maybe one day I could bond with Lotus." It wasn't enough, and it wasn't certain, and it was

going to take far too long—but it was a chance.
She'd never wanted anything so much in her whole
life.

Karis studied her closely. "Normally, my
answer would be no. You come from an important
family, so you already have a way to make your
mark in this world."

Not like this one. She met the older woman's
eyes, hoping she could read what lived in
Sapphire's heart. "My sisters all have special
talents, but I've never had any. I'm entirely
ordinary."

A long pause while the older warrior studied
her. "How old are you, child?"

Sapphire bristled—she hadn't been a child for
years now. "I passed fourteen at the last harvest
moon."

Karis's eyebrows flew up. "I wouldn't have
taken you for more than ten or eleven."

The story of her life. Undersized and
uninteresting. "I'm stronger than you think, and I
don't mind working hard."

An amused chuckle greeted her words. "We
don't judge character on size around here,
youngling—there's no need to take offense."

They'd never let her stay if she couldn't stop

sounding so foolish. Sapphire looked up and met Karis's gaze directly. "My clan is important to me, but there are many in my family, and truly not enough work to keep everyone busy and out of my mother's hair." Or so she said on a regular basis, anyhow. "I think they'd be proud that I found something useful to do." Grandfather's tales of dragons hadn't been very specific, but from what she remembered, he'd held them in high esteem.

"Well, there's no lack of work to do around here." Karis's eyes sharpened. "Have you been schooled?"

"Of course." Sapphire almost bit off her tongue as she heard the sharp tone in her voice. "Moon Clan prides itself on raising elves who are well versed in history, poetry, woodcraft, and the arts." She sighed and figured she'd better tell the truth now before they had time for their opinion of her to improve. "I'm better at some of those than others."

"Aren't we all." The warrior gave a light shrug that carried just the faintest hint of respect. "You come from a family where you're likely quite used to others serving many of your needs."

Finally — something where she could give the right answer and have it be absolute truth. "Not at all. One of the ways my mother tried to keep us out of her hair was to make sure we could all take care of our own needs as far as we were able. I've washed all my own clothes since I was big enough to wade in the river without falling over, I'm a fair hand with a needle and thread, although not as good as some of my sisters, and only my brother Fellin is a better cook over an open fire." She paused, somewhat embarrassed. They probably didn't care that she could make excellent roasted vegetables.

Karis seemed cautiously pleased. "That would be helpful."

Sapphire caught the subtle change in the words. The warrior was considering her request — really considering it. She thought hard for a moment and decided to offer up more of the truth. The dragon kin woman seemed oddly drawn to it. "I'm a bit weak on woodcraft, though. I get lost really easily — that's how I ended up in your hatching grounds."

"Part of it, anyhow." Karis didn't seem inclined to explain her mysterious answer. "And if you end up kin, you'll never need to worry about getting lost. Dragons have a sense of direction no elf or human can match."

Sapphire hadn't made it much past the part about how she might get to bond with a dragon one day. "I can stay?"

"I don't know." Karis's eyes offered more hope than her words. "You seem honest and reasonably aware of your own strengths and failings, and those are both things we value around here. I'll speak to some of the others and decide if we'd like to petition your clan on your behalf."

That sounded complicated. And expensive. Negotiations between clans always were. "I don't know if they'll pay you much to take me." Father was the toughest deal maker this side of the Summerlands, or at least that's what everyone in Moon Clan thought. When he sent fosterlings to other clans, it was always the other side that left the deal circle scowling.

Karis snorted. "You've a very undervalued sense of your own worth for an elf."

That didn't make sense. "I'm the youngest daughter, and very ordinary."

A long, pregnant pause, and then the warrior reached out and laid a strong hand over Sapphire's. "You found a dragon, youngling. Whatever else you are, you're not remotely ordinary."

Sapphire blinked. "I was lost in the forest." Then she remembered about the Mirror—but maybe the spell didn't bother with very ordinary, very lost elves. "I don't have any magic, either, if that's what you're thinking." Very few elves did anymore. Only the ones in the ancient stories.

Karis opened her mouth to say something else, but stopped at the sound of running feet.

A young boy came flying through the door like the hounds of hell were running at his heels. "Irin says to bring Sapphire right now!"

Karis was on her feet before the child finished speaking. "He's in the nursery?" She waved a sharp hand at Sapphire, and a totally unnecessary one. She was already on her feet and following the boy out the door. There was only one reason anyone in this village would have called for her.

"The baby dragon's throwing a gore-awful tantrum," the messenger gasped as he ran. "She near melted one of Irin's favorite swords that he was polishing, and she bit Kis on the nose when he tried to get her to calm down."

Karis looked more amused than concerned as she huffed beside them. "Fierce little thing, is she? How many languages has Irin cursed in so far?"

"At least four." The boy's eyes widened. "But one of them was Dwarvish."

Karis grimaced. "That's not one he pulls out often."

Sapphire was barely listening anymore. She pulled ahead of the other two, panic lending speed to her feet. She could hear a very familiar, very loud yowling coming straight out the door of the biggest rondo.

Her dragon was calling.

Chapter 6

Sapphire didn't even slow down when she barreled into the nursery rondo—she charged right over to where a huge man with a scruffy beard was corralling a hissing-mad peach-pink dragonet high up on a shelf in the corner, and ducked under his right arm.

And then squealed as she felt herself lifted into the air.

"Just slow down there, missy." The man's voice matched his size. He set her down beside him none too gently. "She's been flaming anyone who tries to get close to her nest."

She looked at the woven branches that must be the nest, set up on a ledge at about the height of her chin. "It's too high—she wants to be on the floor." Sapphire didn't know how she knew that, but she could feel the truth of it blazing out of the small, hissing dragon.

"On the floor?" The big man sounded poleaxed. "They never want to be on the floor."

"Lotus does." Sapphire felt very sure. "She's afraid of high places."

"That's impossible. Dragons fly higher than anything else in the world."

Sapphire didn't know anything about that — she only knew about one dragon. "She spent the whole night in the forest with me up in a really big tree and now she's scared and she wants to come down." She could totally sympathize — she wasn't climbing anything higher than a step stool ever again.

"She'd be a strange one if that's what's got her riled." The man didn't seem to disbelieve her, though. He stretched a hand toward Lotus, and yanked it back as a stream of fire shot out her nose. "Can you calm her down enough for me to lift her down?"

Sapphire lifted her chin up. Lotus was *her* dragon. "I can get her down." It couldn't be any harder than climbing down the tree. She took a step toward the shelf, holding her hands up like tree branches, and then jumped back as the next stream of fire nearly scorched her eyebrows off.

"She's got a temper, this one." The man, who must be Irin, sounded like he approved.

Sapphire felt her chest swelling with pride. She could hear the others standing behind her, the quiet accompaniment of their shuffling footsteps and low voices. She ignored them all. Only one thing mattered in this moment, and that was the feeling beating out of the tiny dragonet. "She's tough, but she's scared, too."

"Scared?" The big man beside her didn't sound like he believed a word, but he squatted down beside her on the dirt. "That's a lot of piss and fire to be fear."

"She's terrified." Sapphire held out her hands, palms up. "I'm right here, beautiful."

Lotus started to quiver.

"I bet you need some food for that hungry belly of yours, hmm?" Sapphire wasn't even sure what words she was saying, but she pushed as much calm and soothing at Lotus as she could. "I had mushroom stew last night, but I bet that's not what they fed you."

Green eyes were watching her now.

A voice behind her started to say something and was quickly hushed.

"There are curds in the bowl on the small table

to your right," said the big man in a low rumble she could barely hear.

Lotus hissed again.

"He's a friend." Sapphire kept up the calm, soothing river of words. "He's been trying to help you and get you something to eat, and you've been making a big mess and setting things on fire."

She imagined that the green eyes looked just the tiniest bit embarrassed. Which was silly, because babies didn't understand how much disruption they caused for everyone else. Slowly, Sapphire reached for the copper bowl to her right. "If you're hungry, you can come over here and use your nice dragon manners and we'll see what we can do about fixing that." One more time, she held up her arm like a tree branch, and held her breath as Lotus quivered on the edge of the shelf.

Nothing moved — and then everything moved as baby dragon claws scurried down Sapphire's arm and straight down her tunic to the floor.

Hissing like a wild thing, Lotus backed into the corner.

"Well, that wasn't the most graceful climb, but it will do." Sapphire thought she might have about a hundred holes poked in her, but it didn't matter. Lotus wasn't feeling nearly so scared anymore — just hungry and tired and frazzled, and those were a lot easier to fix.

She took a step closer to the corner, pausing as her dragon blew fire again.

"Careful." Irin was still there, a firm presence in the shadows. "That was well done, but it might take her a while to calm down, and the babies don't understand that we're not fireproof like they are."

"She won't burn me." Sapphire knew it as certainly as her own name. She crouched down on her knees and settled into the warm dirt and kept flowing her words at the frazzled creature in the corner. "That's better. That was far too much noise to be making so early in the morning. You'll need to learn some manners, little one. Big people get cranky if they don't get enough sleep."

The man beside her snorted, but he didn't say a word.

Lotus gazed at him with baleful eyes and let out a fiery hiss.

"That's just about enough out of you," he said, but his voice didn't carry any menace.

Sapphire put some curds on her fingertips and held them out, smiling as Lotus stretched out her whole body to try to reach them without moving her feet. "Come over here and get them, silly."

Tiny dragon claws dragged forward in the dirt just far enough to reach the curds.

Sapphire sat very still, humming a small lullaby about moons and shadows and goddesses in the night.

The next time Lotus took a curd, she didn't back up. Instead, she walked over to Sapphire's lap like she'd always planned to go there and curled up just like a kitten. And then made a yowling noise that Sapphire hastily interpreted as a request for more curds. The whole bowl full. NOW.

Nobody moved as the tiny dragon mowed through her body weight of the soft white chunks. When the bowl was entirely empty, Irin took it from Sapphire's grasp and then carefully reached out a finger toward the dragonet's chin.

Lotus hissed — no fire this time, but her meaning was plenty clear.

"Well. This is a bit of a tangle." Karis crouched down beside Irin. "I've never seen a hatchling who didn't want to have anything to do with you."

"Hatching trauma, perhaps," said a deep voice from behind them who sounded like Sapphire's least favorite teacher back in Moon Clan.

Irin snorted. "Are you all blind? These two are bonded. I'll stake my last sharp sword on it."

Karis raised an eyebrow. "You think?"

"You've got eyes, don't you?" Irin waved a hand at Lotus, nestling into the crook in Sapphire's arm. "You think some random elf girl walked out of the forest and got a baby dragon well on her way to sleep without knowing anything about anything?"

Sapphire wanted to protest — she wasn't entirely useless. "I've had some practice with my little cousins."

Irin snorted again. "Unless they're dragons, I can promise you that isn't why this particular ball of fire is falling asleep in your lap. I've been wrangling babies for nigh on twenty winters now, and that little girl is a spitfire. She trusts you because she's chosen you as her kin."

Something warm lit and spread in Sapphire's chest as she ran a finger over Lotus's eye ridges. Slowly, the baby dragon's eyes began to close.

"Like I said." The old swordsman's voice was gruff, but she imagined she could hear kindness underneath. "She doesn't know a darn thing about dragons, and one's gone and bonded with her anyhow."

"Elhen may have something to say about that." The voice from the doorway was stern and unyielding. Everyone in the nursery turned as one. Even Sapphire managed to swivel her head around to see. The man was tall and slender and carried himself with the bearing of one who expected instant obedience at all times.

"Hello, Morigen." Irin stepped forward, his body language showing respect, but not awe. "It's not often we see you in these parts."

"I've just returned from the southlands," said the new arrival. "Ciara bade Ness to pass a message to the nursery, so I've come to do so."

One of Irin's helpers jumped to her feet, heading for the door. "I'll get Ness some food and water."

The man nodded his head at the girl. "That would be appreciated." He looked over, straight into Sapphire's eyes. "For the rest of you, the queen requires your presence. She wishes to meet the two new arrivals."

Chapter 7

Sapphire was pretty sure she was supposed to be more scared than she was feeling, at least based on the awed glances she was getting from Kellan, who had taken up a position on her left side. Even Karis, on her other side, was walking like someone in a parade processional, the kind where there would be people on the sides of the path to wave to at any minute.

Sapphire had walked in plenty of processionals. As the youngest daughter of Moon Clan's ruling family, she'd also met plenty of queens and other royalty. Mostly it was boring, with lots of speeches, fancy clothes, and the kind of manners that made her itch the whole time she had to use them.

She tried to keep her grumpy thoughts from

growing too big. This was the adventure of her lifetime, and she didn't want to ruin it inside her own head. For all she knew, someone from her clan could come get her at any minute, and there was so much she hadn't seen yet. Lotus was calm for the moment, perched on her shoulder and quietly chirruping as they walked, and Sapphire wanted everyone to see how well they did together.

Maybe then they would let her stay.

Lotus, craning her head around, made a surprised sound, her eyes wide and curious. Kellan followed the green-eyed gaze and smiled. "Those are barracks for visiting dragons and their kin." She talked right to Lotus, as if the dragonet could understand every word she said. "Some of us live here in the village year round, but most are out on tour. This is where they stay when they come to report in and catch up on their sleep."

The barracks looked like several rondos had all been squished together. Now that it wasn't raining so hard, Sapphire could make out the dragon-sized entrances, and the ones that were probably for guests of the two-legged variety. "What do they do out on tour?"

"Hrrmph." Irin strode up beside them, grunting. "It'd be shorter to list what they *don't* do. Some pairs are soldiers or peacekeepers, some mediate land disputes, some map out new routes or escort trade caravans or dig for treasure."

Sapphire blinked at the last. "Dig where?"

"Into mountains, mostly. Looking for jewels, ore, precious metals."

"Miner dragons." Kellan had stars in her eyes. "I think that's what Kyrn wants to be."

"You know better than to set your eye on a dragon before you've bonded," Irin said gruffly.

"Kyrn loves finding pretty things." Kellan made a face behind the old warrior's back.

"Aye, that he does." The master of the nursery was still speaking with the voice of a soldier, but Sapphire could see something more like sympathy in his eyes. "But that doesn't mean he'll be yours, missy."

"I know that." Kellan's eyes snapped dark fire. "Maybe no dragon will bond with me at all and I'll have done all this work for nothing and I'll have to leave and go be a wandering bard or something."

The old soldier nodded like she'd said all that in a perfectly civil tone. "Could happen. Being a bard might suit you, should it come to that. Kis likes it well enough when you sing to him."

"Kis is old and half deaf."

Irin chuckled. "So are most of the men in taverns."

Sapphire listened to the conversation between them with no small astonishment. If she'd spoken like that to any of the clan elders, she'd have found herself on floor-scrubbing duty for the rest of her natural life. Kellan clearly had a temper and wasn't afraid to let it fly.

Maybe waiting for a dragon did that to you.

Sapphire leaned her ear against Lotus, sighing as a warm head leaned back. She had a dragon, if only she could convince anyone else to believe it.

Maybe Irin did — and that was a start.

The landscape was changing around them. They'd moved off the flat paths of the village proper and were climbing a gentle incline. Some large boulders sat in the mosses, but no trees. It felt oddly exposed compared to the lush forests of Moon Clan territory.

"There are caves up here," Kellan said quietly. "Some of the older dragons prefer them to the rondos."

Irin snorted. "They prefer some peace and quiet away from noisy younglings, you mean."

There were elves like that in Moon Clan — elders who had given of their gifts and now just wanted to sleep and watch the moon travel through the night sky. Sapphire had always felt vaguely sad for them.

"They come." Karis stepped up beside her, pointing off in the distance. "Afran is in the lead."

Sapphire squinted, her mind still distracted by thoughts of home. All she saw were a couple of dots on the horizon.

And then there were more dots, and bigger ones.

"A lot today." Irin grunted and shot a glance at Kis, lumbering painfully up the hill beside them. "I knew there must be a reason you wanted to come, old man."

Kellan had just plain stopped, staring up at the sky, mouth wide open. "I've never seen so many in all my life."

Sapphire could feel the unease building in her own heart—and the excitement building in Lotus, who was squeezing far too tightly with her claws and craning her neck to see. "What's going on?"

"Dragons and their kin," Kellan whispered. "More than I've ever seen, coming to pay their respects to the queen. Some of them must have been flying for days to be here."

Sapphire watched, dumbfounded, as the spots grew bigger and blacker, a great huge swarm of them. Her legs got the strange jelly feeling again, just like when she'd finally made it out of the tree. She could make out individual dragons now, Afran in the lead, by far the biggest in the swarm.

She reminded herself that he had kind eyes.

Which almost worked — until she met the fierce, curious gazes of some of the new dragons as they landed. Her heart plummeted into her boots.

They came in every color of the rainbow, and even some she hadn't known existed. Brilliant glowing scales, huge wings fine enough to let the daylight pass through and mighty enough to hurtle through the air and screech to a stop less than an elf-length from the ground, and puffs of smoke and flame everywhere she looked.

And sliding off their backs, riders in every size and shape of imagining. Elf and human, young and old, people as thick as tree trunks and as ethereal as butterflies.

As one, the riders stepped to the heads of their dragons and bowed.

To her.

Kellan sucked in an awed breath.

Sapphire felt her leg wobbles turn into an earthquake.

"Have a care, missy." Irin's hand clamped on her shoulder, holding her up and holding her still all at the same time. "It's great respect they're showing you and the hatchling. I assume you've got some manners in that head of yours, and now's the right time to be showing them."

Manners. Royalty.

Sapphire almost let loose a hysterical giggle. To think she'd been thinking this would be boring — and they hadn't even gotten to the queen yet.

She did, however, have enough of a mind left to know that Irin was wrong. The dragons couldn't possibly be here to meet the youngest daughter of Moon Clan, which must mean that Lotus was very important.

Carefully, waiting for the baby dragon's claws to find purchase, Sapphire raised her arm so everyone could see Lotus and cleared her throat. Projecting her voice just like Grandfather had taught her, she spoke to Afran's kind eyes. "Her name is Lotus, and she's very honored to meet all of you."

Lotus sat up very straight and chirruped at the top of her lungs.

The skies rumbled as the assembled dragons replied.

Lotus's eyes bulged as big as dinner plates, and then every dragon head turned as one, looking to a high ledge off to Sapphire's left. Two dragons stood on the edge, surveying the gathered crowd.

"The guardians." Kellan had found her voice again, but it was still hushed with awe. "The queen can see through their eyes."

Sapphire blinked. "Why doesn't she come out if all these dragons came to honor her?"

Irin snorted. "She's old as these hills, missy. It's worth more than my hide or yours to be trying to move her. The guardians act as her eyes and ears, and they'll relay anything she says to those who don't fit inside."

Karis laughed. "Today, that will be pretty much everyone. Elhen likes her space, and Afran says they've all been told to stay outside."

Sapphire swallowed. She had so much to learn about dragons. Like how they were managing to do all this talking that she couldn't hear.

An awful thought landed. Maybe you didn't get to bond with a dragon unless you could hear them.

"Come." Irin's hand was back on her shoulder. "The queen awaits."

Legs still trembling, Sapphire tried to walk as she'd been taught — with dignity and grace and the knowledge that everyone was looking and would report the tiniest misstep.

Lotus bumped her head against Sapphire's

chest and then preened for the audience, chirruping quietly.

Irin chuckled. "Well, good thing one of you isn't shy."

Sapphire just watched Karis's back in front of her and kept walking. So many fierce eyes. She took a deep breath and looked into the only ones that mattered.

The sweet green eyes of her dragon.

Sapphire straightened as they walked into the mouth of the cave. Dragon kin came in all kinds of shapes and sizes, and not all of them could possibly be fierce. She wanted to stay so very badly, and this might be her best chance. She knew just how much weight a royal opinion could carry.

They walked a little deeper into the shadows, moving slowly, and then the space opened up and something cast a lovely yellow glow, and Sapphire's eyes could see again. She looked around for a fire, but she couldn't see one. The cave was very warm, but if her cheeks were telling her right, the heat seemed to come mostly from the shimmery guardian dragons, one on each side of the cave. The queen herself was almost translucent, an eerie white shadow that picked up color from everything around her. A ghost dragon—and one who didn't appear to have a head.

Karis stepped forward and cleared her throat.

"Elhen, we have come as commanded."

For a long moment, nothing in the cave moved. Then a low, rumbling voice spoke from under the queen's tail. "It wasn't a command, child — nothing more than a polite request."

Karis looked amused. "In that case, we have come as requested." She waited as a large head emerged from under the tail, and then motioned Sapphire up beside her. "This is Sapphire of Moon Clan, and the hatchling she rescued from up a tree in the breeding grove."

A large, translucent eyebrow slid up the queen's eye ridges. "And what fool brooder laid their egg in a tree, pray tell?"

"We don't know." Karis shrugged uncomfortably. "Afran believes it might not have started there."

That was news to Sapphire.

"Well, the egg surely didn't climb on its own." Elhen directed a sharp stare at everyone in the cave. "The breeding grove is sacred. It always has been." Her eyes settled on Sapphire's shoulder. "Perhaps the young one knows how her egg came to be there."

Lotus pushed her head back into Sapphire's chest.

Sapphire shook her head mutely. Neither of them knew anything.

"Ah, well. Perhaps that is not the part of the story that matters." Elhen gazed on the two of them, and Sapphire felt like she was being seen right down to her very soul. The queen finally nodded, very slowly, and when she spoke again, her words took on the feel of portent. "What matters is that you are one of the five."

The hush in the cave was remarkable and total.

The queen's blue-green eyes glistened with something that almost looked like tears. "It begins. In my lifetime, it begins."

It was Irin who finally broke the silence. "Honored one, I have to ask — are you certain?"

"They are marked." The rumble wavered, and then firmed again. "It was said that the queen would see their markings. There is a light on each of their foreheads. Can you not see it?"

Sapphire quivered under the burning gazes of everyone in the cave. She couldn't see anything — not on Lotus, anyhow. And her own forehead felt the same way it always had.

"She won't know the story," Karis said quietly, stepping up to Sapphire's shoulder. "Perhaps you would share it with us once again."

Elhen nodded regally. "These are the words that have been told, passed down from queen to queen, beginning with Lovissa, the great warrior dragon. She is the grandmother of my grandmother, twenty-five generations past. This is the story that has been passed from Lovissa to me."

Sapphire was quite certain that everyone else in the cave knew this story. As they should. Clan history was a clan's greatest treasure, or so she had always been taught. She just didn't have any idea how it could possibly apply to her. She listened to the words wrapping around her, the tale of battles won and lost and dragonkind at the very brink of disappearing from the world forever, brought down from the skies by terrible magics and storms of arrows that pierced wings and stopped dragon hearts forever.

Sapphire could feel the tears streaming down her cheeks. It was elves who had done this. That didn't seem possible. Elves honored peace.

Lotus's heart beat fast against her chest.

"It did not end the way the dragons of old feared," Elhen intoned. "We do not know the full story of how they were saved, for that has been lost in the fires of time. But the wisdom of the queens has passed on this much. There will be five who come to save all dragonkind. And they will be marked by a light that shines just above their eyes."

She looked at Sapphire and Lotus expectantly.

The hush in the cave was absolute.

Sapphire smiled tremulously. She knew what the light was now — or at least she knew who had put it there. "It was the Dragon Star. She touched us in a dream."

"Just so." Elhen seemed delighted. She looked at Irin and Karis and spoke sharply. "The girl will remain, of course. And you will train them as thoroughly as you have ever trained a dragon and her kin. They must be ready for what comes. As must we all."

That sounded big. And scary. And dangerous. But as a very sleepy Lotus cuddled into Sapphire's chest, she also knew it meant one very important thing.

She was allowed to stay.

Lotus was hers.

Interlude

Lovissa woke with a snort. She could feel the tears running down her scales, dripping onto the floor of her cave. Such a dream. Or rather, a vision, for she had no doubt but that she had seen true. Through the eyes of the daughter of her daughter's daughter, five times five generations hence.

And such a story she had told.

Lovissa's heart burned hot with gratitude, for the vision had spoken to her greatest fear. Dragonkind was indeed in grave danger — but there would be a way. There would be dragons stretching down for generations far beyond this time, and led by such a one as she could be so very proud of. Elhen's resonance of voice, her clarity of mind, the farseeing wisdom — such a queen. Such a granddaughter.

Telling a story Lovissa could scarcely believe.

For while her very scales still recoiled at some of what she had seen, she could not avoid the truth held in the minds of the dragons in Elhen's cave. Young and old, large and small, their minds spoke the same truth. They were fulfilled. Satisfied. Living lives of purpose as every dragon sought to do. Time might change much, but it pleased her greatly to know it would not change that.

Because it would change everything else.

She shivered as the echoes of dragon mind memory resonated in the part of her that had known she was meant to be queen even before she had hatched. So much that was different.

Some of the changes were ones she embraced with the fire of pure joy. The purpose she had sensed in the gathered dragons – that place where they each chose to focus their lives – caught Lovissa's breath in her lungs because in all that she had heard, and all that she had seen, there had been only a single warrior.

Old and fierce to be sure – but only one.

For a queen who had watched so many brave dragons die, that alone was a message of wrenching hope. She had lost so many. Warriors by necessity instead of life's purpose. For there to come a time when they might seek their soul's true purpose and not sacrifice themselves on the fires of battle – she would rejoice greatly to know such a time came for dragonkind.

Even if they must live side-by-side with their sworn enemies.

Lovissa could feel the fear of that quaking in her belly. What must come to pass before a dragon would close their eyes in the same cave as an elf? To sleep, while the enemy polished their knives?

And yet, she had seen it in the memories of those who gathered round the queen. Clear as day, from dragon and elf both. Camaraderie. Trust.

To share such with an elf was unthinkable.

And yet.

She had seen, as was her duty — and she would not turn away.

Lovissa climbed ponderously to her feet and strode as gracefully as she could to the cave's entrance. She perched on the edge of the rocky cliff and raised her wings into the night sky. The deeper meaning of the child seeking and an egg left precariously in a tree had not been lost on her. Always, legends and dreams were full of such symbols, and it was the queen's place to understand them.

It was not her job to find the five. They would come when it was their time, making their strange and difficult journeys, called by what lived in their hearts and marked by the Dragon Star.

Her job was not to find them, or to keep them safe. It was to make sure her dragons were ready.

To begin the story that would one day be told by

Elhen to the first of the five. She would pass on every word of what she had seen, every scrap of detail in her dream. Her old eyes had been as cunning as they could possibly be. When the moment was right, she would share that knowledge with the dragons of the Veld.

She would tell them of Sapphire and Lotus. It was so very hard to entrust the future of dragonkind into such young claws — but trust she must. Lovissa held their names within her core of fire and felt it burn bright, felt the calling of what she must do.

Elhen had spoken truly. It had begun.

PART II:

Eating Dirt

Chapter 8

"Free at last."

Sapphire laughed as her best friend scooted out the door of the rondo that served as their classroom, dancing her way into the late-afternoon light. Kellan worked harder at her studies than any of them, but she hated sitting still, and Karis had made them sit a long time that day.

Lily rubbed her bottom ruefully. "I think I'm numb."

Alonia snorted. "That's because you're all bony and you never eat enough to feed a flea."

"*Someone* never leaves anything on the platter by the time it gets to my end of the table."

Alonia grinned and patted her own substantial

bottom, covered by a pretty green dress. "I have to watch my figure, you know. Dragons like a comely lass."

Lily rolled her eyes. "Dragons like someone with half a brain in their head."

Sapphire let the banter wash over her. Two years of listening to them tease each other had made her immune — and if anyone else ever said an unkind word to either Lily or Alonia, the other one would be first in line to throw a punch. They fought like sisters, and she'd been well used to that as the youngest of eight of them.

Kellan danced her way back to Sapphire's side, rolling her eyes at their two classmates. "I think they've gotten worse since Dinny and Morris left."

The two boys had just graduated and left the village, Dinny on his first tour with Lyris, and Morris off to seek his way in the world until a dragon or a woman came and dragged him off — or at least that's what he'd said as he made his jaunty way out of the village and off to the big city. It had left a distinct hole in their class. All the other boys in the village were much younger and barely counted as people, at least as far as flirtatious Alonia was concerned. She came from a clan that handfasted young and had many children, and living in a village with no resident boys her age left a gap in her life that needed filling.

Sapphire hoped it was a dragon who filled it, and not a new arrival. Her sisters had always been fixated on some boy or another, and she'd had enough of it to fill a lifetime.

There were so many other fun things they could be doing instead. She looked at the three who had become the closest thing she had to family in the last two years and offered up her best idea for how to spend a free afternoon. "I stopped by the apple orchard yesterday, and I think if we pick carefully, we can get enough to make a pie." She eyed Kellan. "If someone will bake it for us."

Kellan laughed. "One day, you three are going to be out on tour, and you're going to starve."

Sapphire cooked just fine, but teasing didn't have to be true to be funny. "Inga says Lily can almost boil water now."

Lily snorted. "I hardboiled the eggs you had for dinner last night and nobody died."

Alonia clutched her stomach and made a gagging noise.

Kellan laughed and elbowed Sapphire in the ribs. "If you helped Inga more, maybe she wouldn't need to recruit Lily the Water Burner."

"That's a good idea." Alonia's eyes were bright with merriment. "Inga says I eat too much when I help, and that Lily's as cranky as a cat in an empty fish pond."

Lily scowled. "I'd take the fish pond any day. It's too hot in the kitchens. It makes me feel all dry and scaldy."

Sapphire had no idea how Lily survived at a dragon village at all. She was a water elf through and through, always splashing in a river or lake or even a bucket of water. She seemed like the last person likely to bond with a dragon, but all the dragons of the village loved her, even when she scolded them for making fire breath anywhere in her vicinity.

Lily might have a sharp tongue, but she had a heart of gold, and in this small village, there was no way to hide it.

Sapphire turned left, intending to herd everyone toward the apple orchard — until she felt the mind touch that meant Lotus was near.

Very near. Sapphire focused her attention long enough to register the glee in her dragon's mind, and then groaned and started pushing at her friends. "Get under cover — quick."

"Oh, no. Not again." Kellan took off for a rain barrel tucked under an eave. Water was excellent dragon repellant.

Lily grabbed the much-slower Alonia's hand, half dragging her to the nearest open doorway.

Sapphire splayed herself against the classroom rondo wall and tried to send calming thoughts to her incoming dragon. *::Slow down. If you break anything, Karis will make us pick rocks in the cow pasture for the next week.::*

Their bond transmitted feelings a lot better than it did words, but it was better than doing nothing. Or maybe not. Two-year-old dragons tended to ignore pretty much anything that wasn't on fire or edible.

Sapphire didn't need Kellan's pointing arm to tell her that she'd failed.

Lotus came into view at the edge of the village, neck and wings and tail stretched out in wild abandon. She zoomed just over the rondo rooftops and then shot down the wide path that wound through most of the village, her claws no more than three feet off the ground.

Sapphire gave up trying to mindspeak and yelled instead. "Up, Lotus. Go higher!"

Her dragon turned happy green eyes her way and shifted course.

Oh, no. She was headed straight for them now. Sapphire watched the incoming peach-pink wings and ducked. This had been a lot cuter when Lotus was small. Back in those days, everyone had laughed and offered her a handful of milk curds. They'd had no idea they were training the village menace.

Kellan, perched on top of a water barrel, eyed the flying terror as Lotus zoomed off into the distance and sighed. "Three feet higher and she wouldn't be taking off all our heads."

Higher was the problem. Lotus had learned to fly before her first birthday, just like every other baby dragon—but she had a terrible fear of heights. Sapphire knew why. A long, cold night up a tree on the night of her hatching had left them both with a very strong preference for having their feet on the ground. Or in Lotus's case, close enough to get there really quickly if necessary.

Which didn't preclude showing off her barrel rolls right through the middle of the village.

Sapphire stepped out into the central path and waited. It was only a matter of time before a certain reckless dragon circled back around, unable to resist the lure of an audience and the unintentional wind tunnel the main path through the village created—if you were a small dragon without a lick of common sense, anyhow.

"Here she comes," Kellan hissed from behind her rain barrel.

Sapphire didn't question her best friend— Kellan had ears like a fox.

A moment later, she could hear Lotus

approaching herself. Sapphire reached inside for the deep connection she shared with the peach-pink winged monster and tried to wrap her in calm discipline. She also projected as much disapproval as she could. Lotus might be acting like a teenager, but under her harebrained exterior, she was mostly still a sensitive hatchling who lapped up love almost as fast as she ate milk curds — and she hated it when Sapphire was mad at her.

Dragons who could fly weren't supposed to get milk curds anymore, but no one in the village had the heart to cut her off. Although that might change if the barrel roll fly-bys didn't stop soon. Sapphire held up her palms as a peach-colored streak came winging around Karis's rondo and headed straight at her.

It took all the courage she had not to close her eyes and drop to the ground as Lotus hurtled closer. She knew her dragon would never hurt her on purpose, but there was one flying skill Lotus definitely hadn't mastered yet, and that was stopping.

A heavy ball of dragon smacked into her outstretched arms and knocked both of them into a tumbling pile in the dirt. Sapphire cursed as her leg crashed into something hard. When they finally came to a stop, she figured out which way was the ground and pushed herself up to sitting. "Darn it, Lotus — you know you're not supposed to fly through the village." That wasn't a rule any other dragon needed, but it hadn't taken long for the residents to vote it into local law.

Lotus hunched over in the dirt a few feet away, looking dusty and chastened.

Sapphire was smart enough not to believe it. If she turned her back, she was pretty sure the next fly-by would happen before she had time to dust off her leggings. "We're both going to be in big trouble when Karis hears about this."

"That's already happened," said a dry voice from behind her.

Lotus hunched over further, doing her best impression of a tiny, guiltless hatchling.

Karis walked over and squatted by the small dragon. "I'm onto you, terrible creature. Afran says you have enough energy inside you to keep a dozen dragons flying for a whole moon cycle."

Kellan and Lily snickered from nearby.

Sapphire was smart enough not to laugh. This was her dragon in trouble, and whatever consequences landed on Lotus generally heaped onto both of them. "She's just a baby."

"No, she's not," Karis said briskly, swiveling around gracefully in her crouch. "She's all wings and no brains, and we're used to that around here. We're just not used to it flying quite so close over our heads."

Sapphire winced. Every dragon in the village had tried to help Lotus fly higher, and most of the human and elf inhabitants too. "She'll figure it out once she gets a little bigger." Maybe.

"Afran doesn't think so."

That wasn't good. The wise old dragon was gentle and kind and had helped Sapphire through sadness more than once in the last two years, but he was also really fixed in his ways. Once he made up his mind about something, it rarely changed.

He was also hardly ever wrong. "What does that mean?" Sapphire couldn't imagine what it would be like for Lotus never to fly properly. She knew that her dragon was sad in her dreams sometimes, wanting to be up high like the others.

"We have to be able to fix this." Kellan sat down cross-legged beside Sapphire and offered a cup of water from the rain barrel.

Karis smiled at the younger girl. "It's good that you're always thinking of how to help others. I believe that will be seen as your greatest strength one day."

Kellan made a face. "After people stop seeing me as a little kid, you mean."

Sapphire knew her best friend got tired of

being the baby of the village. And she knew that what was really going on had nothing to do with size or age or anything like that. Kellan wanted to bond with a dragon as much as she wanted to breathe, but despite living at the village most of her life and being well known to all of the dragons, not one of them had ever shown any signs of making Kellan their kin.

Which wasn't fair, especially when Sapphire felt guilty about bonding with the first dragon she'd ever laid eyes on. She reached over and wrapped an arm around Kellan's shoulders.

Karis watched them both with approval in her eyes. "Afran has an idea, and I think it has merit."

All Afran's ideas had merit. Sapphire looked over at Lotus, who was listening intently and using her long tongue to clean the dust off her scales. She grinned — her dragon liked to keep herself all shiny. Most dragons did. It reminded her of her sisters back in Moon Clan, primping and prettying all day long.

Karis reached out and scratched the spot under Lotus's chin that was always itchy. "We're not used to having dragons who have bonded so young, and perhaps it has made us overlook the obvious."

Whatever it was still wasn't obvious to Sapphire, but she knew enough not to interrupt

Karis. Their teacher could be long winded sometimes, especially when she was sharing the thought processes of her dragon. Afran always got to the end point, but he tended to take long and circuitous roads to get there.

Their teacher swept her gaze over all of them again, and then nodded decisively. "Afran believes that Lotus may learn to fly better with you on her back."

Sapphire could feel the blood rushing out of her head. She looked at Lotus, stupefied. "You want me to ride her while she does those crazy barrel rolls?" That was several vales beyond insane.

"No." Karis looked amused. "I want you to ride her while you practice some very sedate maneuvers with Afran over the south fields."

That was where they taught all the baby dragons to fly. Wide-open flat spaces and soft landings.

Karis laid a hand on Kellan's shoulder. "As you are a calming presence for both Sapphire and Lotus, Afran requests your assistance. He says that you may fly on his back during the lessons, and he would welcome your thoughtful input."

All the protests Sapphire had been lining up died abruptly as she watched wild joy bloom on her best friend's face.

Dragons hardly ever flew anyone other than their kin. That Afran had decided to make an exception was huge. None of them wanted to think about it, but Kellan might never bond. She might never have a dragon of her own to ride. She might never get this chance again — and no way was Sapphire going to take it from her.

Even if it meant barrel rolling into the soft dirt of the south fields every day for a year.

Chapter 9

It was the perfect day for apple picking or taking a picnic to the river or hanging laundry outside to dry. The afternoon sun was giving strong hints of summer to come, and it warmed the top of Sapphire's head and the back of her neck. The rest of her was wearing as much padding as she'd been able to find on short notice because Karis and Afran had decided it was also the perfect day for a flying lesson.

She looked over at Kellan, who wasn't wearing any padding at all, and looked like there was nothing more in the entire universe that she would rather be doing than walking over to the south fields to climb on the back of a dragon. Then again, that was probably true. Kellan had been up since the crack of dawn, baking special meat pies for Afran.

Sapphire had been up since the crack of dawn too, but she'd spent her morning sweeping and cleaning and repairing a rain barrel and generally trying to right the damage Lotus had done on her wild flights through the village the day before. Sadly, dragons couldn't hold a broom, although she'd been sorely tempted to tie one to a certain peach-pink tail and demand some help with her penance.

"Don't be grumpy," Kellan said, swinging her basket of meat pies gaily as she walked. "Maybe Lotus will be on her best behavior today, and I bet Afran's the best teacher there is."

It wasn't in Sapphire to dim her best friend's good mood by pointing out the obvious. Lotus was a menace every day of the week, and Afran had been trying to get her more than five feet in the air for almost a year now. Sticking a well-padded elf on her back didn't seem likely to change much. "Maybe."

Kellan grinned. "Are you hungry? I brought extra meat pies."

Dragons weren't the only ones who loved them, but Sapphire's stomach was already feeling queasy. "Maybe after Karis decides I've eaten enough dirt for the day." Everyone else had laughed at her outfit, but there was very little doubt in Sapphire's mind about where this afternoon was headed.

"Karis isn't in charge today," said a cheerful voice behind them. "Afran says I'm to sit quietly and only offer advice if he asks for it."

Sapphire laughed at their long-legged teacher, who'd clearly had no problem catching up to them. "I guess I'm not the only one with a bossy dragon." Although it was hard to imagine that Afran's demands came with insistent, squeaky chirrups loud enough to deafen an entire forest.

"You certainly aren't."

The wry tone made Sapphire want to ask for some stories from when Karis and Afran were younger, but they were almost at the south fields. She looked around for her dragon. Maybe Lotus had gone off on one of her forest gallivants and was scaring birds instead of remembering her flying lesson.

Karis lifted the corner of the cloth covering Kellan's basket. "Someone knows the way to a dragon's heart."

Kellan blushed. "I just wanted to thank Afran for being so kind and letting me ride him today."

"You're not here to be a passenger. He asked for your assistance because he thinks you show uncommon wisdom for one so young."

Sapphire grinned — if Kellan's cheeks got any pinker, she'd fit right in with the apple trees. "He's hoping you'll rub off on me and Lotus."

"Yes, he is." Karis was looking around now too, trying to spot anything resembling a dragon.

Since there were none in sight, Sapphire decided she had time to ask one of the questions that had kept her up most of the night. "Lotus is still pretty small — do you think she's strong enough to carry me?"

"Absolutely." Karis held out her arms. "Have you seen her wingspan? Right now she's all wing and a tiny body, and that makes her the strongest flyer that she'll ever be."

Something about that didn't sound right. "Then why do all the other dragons wait until they're full-grown to fly with their kin?"

Karis sighed. "Because it's generally better to wait for their brains to grow up and match their flying prowess."

Sapphire tried not to groan. Lotus's brain definitely had some growing up to do. And a well-padded rider wasn't likely to make that happen any faster, either, no matter what anyone else thought. *They* weren't bonded to a dragon with the listening skills of a bean sprout.

"There they are." Kellan pointed at two dragons coming around the edge of the woods, one just clearing the trees, the other peeling along about two feet off the ground.

Karis shook her head. "I have no idea how she flies that low. Afran says he would turn us both into road mush if he tried."

This day was just getting better and better. Sapphire checked all her padding and decided it wasn't nearly squishy enough. She would just end up overdressed road mush, and it would take the healers two days to get all her clothes off so they could find her injuries.

Kellan grabbed her hand as Afran and Lotus approached. "It's time."

The awe in her best friend's voice was a living, breathing thing, and it yanked Sapphire out of her woe-is-me thoughts and back into the present. Kellan's fingers gripped hers with the strength of dragon claws, and the younger girl couldn't take her eyes off the two approaching forms. Afran dropped to the ground a polite distance away, barely disturbing the air, and nodded at Kellan. Lotus landed a moment later and kicked up dust all over them.

The bigger dragon glared at the smaller one, and Lotus hung her head.

Sapphire just shook hers. Lotus always felt bad for misbehaving, but she never seemed to remember her regret the next time she had a dumb idea. She would likely dust them all again in five minutes, and look equally chastened after it happened.

Karis dusted off her face and laid a quiet hand on her dragon's huge nose.

Afran rumbled quietly, and Karis grinned. "He says he could smell those meat pies from the other side of the forest."

Kellan nodded, her jaw hanging slack. "I know. I can hear him."

Karis's eyes widened.

Sapphire had never heard of a dragon mind speaking to anyone other than their kin. Most dragons, like Lotus, couldn't speak to anyone.

::For today, I am making an exception.::

The deep voice inside her head was slow and rumbly and exceedingly clear. Sapphire stared.

Afran's eyes glittered with something that looked almost like amusement. ::Your small dragon here doesn't listen very well. We might all eat less dirt if there is at least one of you who will heed my words.::

Lotus rubbed her head up against Afran's leg, in the way of young dragonets to a wise elder.

The larger dragon only snorted.

Sapphire gulped. They all had far more faith in her ability to guide Lotus than she did.

Karis stepped forward and cleared her throat. "All right, let's get you girls up on dragon back." She eyed Kellan. "I generally use Afran's tail to climb up, but I don't know if that will work for you. It's pretty bony and narrow compared to his back, and you have to make quite the jump at the end."

"I can do it." Kellan nearly levitated with excitement. "I've seen you get on him a hundred times, and I know exactly what to do."

"All right, then." Karis smiled at the younger girl and gestured at the big dragon. "Let's see how it goes. You can always have him set you back down if the jump looks too far, and we'll work out a different plan."

Kellan wasn't even listening—she was already moving toward Afran's tail, which lay in a neat semi-circle near his legs. She grabbed hold of a couple of his tail spikes and then hopped up, light as a feather, to crouch between them. "Is this okay?"

She was talking to Afran, but Karis nodded. "You're far more nimble on your feet than I am. Hold tight while he lifts you."

Sapphire was pretty sure the instructions were unnecessary. Kellan had eyes only for the big dragon as he smoothly swept his tail up to the level of his back, and the joy on her face was as radiant as the midsummer sun.

"That girl needs a dragon," Karis said gruffly.

Sapphire nodded, and then clapped wildly as Kellan neatly made the leap from tail to dragon back as if she'd been doing it her whole life.

::That was well done.::

They could all hear Afran's approval. Kellan practically glowed.

"Well." Karis's voice was brisk, but it was clear that she was pleased. "It appears our biggest problem might be getting her down again." She turned to Sapphire. "I expect you can just scramble up if Lotus will crouch down a little for you."

The smaller dragon was already squiggling awkwardly into position, just like she'd seen some of the bigger dragons do for their riders.

Sapphire stepped over to her dragon and put her nose to Lotus's in the way she'd done every day for the last two years. "I love you, even if your ears don't work and you're probably going to break me into a million pieces."

She could feel the warmth streaming back through their bond. Lotus loved her, too — and she was at least as excited and scared and anxious as her rider. Sapphire slid her hand under a peach-pink chin and scratched. They would do their very best and they would do it together, just like they always had right from the beginning.

She walked the two steps to Lotus's shoulder and swung a leg over, settling easily right in front of her wings. She grinned — that part, at least, hadn't been so hard. It was kind of like sitting on a nice, warm, rounded rock.

Then Lotus moved, rising up out of her crouch, and it didn't feel like sitting on a rock at all. Sapphire grabbed a couple of neck spines and held on for dear life.

"Here, try this." Karis moved forward and guided one of Sapphire's feet into the place where Lotus's front legs met her body. "She's small enough that you can tuck your toes in here like this to help you keep your balance."

Sapphire mirrored the motion on the other side and felt a lot more secure — but still not nearly ready to leave the ground.

Karis tilted her head for a moment, listening. "Afran says you're to practice takeoff and landing hops."

Sapphire knew what those were — the first lesson of all baby dragons. Flap just long enough to lift off the ground and then land again. It looked easy when the dragonets did it, but the idea of the big wings behind her starting to flap made her want to throw up the little bit of breakfast she'd managed to eat.

Afran rumbled, and Lotus's head snapped up. Sapphire barely had time to grab hold again before there were three sharp gusts of air behind her and they were lifting up.

Lifting up—and then tipping forward precipitously.

Sapphire screeched and ducked as they plowed into the ground nose first, pluming dust up everywhere.

Then she felt frustration pumping through the dragon underneath her, and before she could catch her breath or say a word, they were back in the air again. This time, they managed to get a little higher before the nose dive happened, which just meant they ate that much more dirt on the landing.

Sapphire tried to send calm to her dragon, and patience, and to tell Lotus that she didn't need to be embarrassed. Learning to fly with a rider was probably really tricky, and she was still just a baby. When Lotus didn't appear to hear any of that, she just tried begging her to stop because Lotus kept hurling them both in the air over and over again, and landing on her nose back in the dirt.

Sapphire had no idea how long they kept it up, how many times they crashed, or how much dust she ate. She only knew that when Lotus finally stopped, head hanging, in the middle of the field, they were both panting like they'd just run for days, her tongue felt like a sand-encrusted desert, and her hands were wrapped so tightly around two neck spikes that she might never pry them off.

She hung her head in shame right alongside her dragon. They might be the worst flyers in dragon history.

A brush of air against her cheek was all the warning she had as Afran landed. Kellan clung to his back, her face full of fear and awe. He looked at the two of them. ::Perhaps now you are ready to stop beating your heads against brick and listen, younglings. It's all in the angle of your wings. Watch.::

One flap of his immense wings, and Afran was in the air. With the grace of one of Moon Clan's finest dancers, Afran pointed his nose at the ground until he seemed almost certain to plow right into it and then lifted it back up, all while hovering ten feet up off the ground. And then he did it again, in the age-old way of teaching that was common to dragons and elves both.

It took Sapphire a while to notice how he was shifting his wings to counterbalance the movements of his body, and even longer for Lotus to start paying attention. But when she did, the despair in their bond started to calm, and in its place came rising excitement.

The small dragon lifted her head, and Sapphire could feel muscles bunching in her back and fierce intention billowing from somewhere deep in her ribcage. Sapphire had just enough time to grab hold more tightly and then they were lifting into the air again—and this time, they stayed there.

They weren't hovering like Afran. They were zooming over the field below, faster than Sapphire had ever gone. She closed her eyes against the blur, feeling horribly dizzy.

It took a while for Kellan's wild, excited whooping from somewhere far above to penetrate.

They were flying. In the sky and not in the dirt. They were doing it. Sapphire forced her eyes back open, not wanting to miss a single moment of their success—just in time to see the world tilt sideways.

Lotus, doing a barrel roll of victory.

Sapphire felt her legs jolt free, her exhausted hands slide off the neck spikes, and saw the earth rushing up to meet her. It didn't look soft at all. Not at this speed. She screamed and curled up into a ball like Irin taught in weapons class and waited to fracture into a million elf pieces.

The claws that grabbed her felt like they came out of nowhere. She stayed curled in a little ball as Afran landed them all in a tidy pile right back where they'd started.

"Well," Karis said dryly. "The two of you might need some practice."

Sapphire groaned. She was never getting on a dragon ever again. She was bruised and battered, her hands felt like they'd been in a boxing match with a mountain, and she'd swallowed enough dust to start her own garden. She was done.

Done, done, done, done, done.

A wet tongue licked her cheek.

She tried to protest — that would just turn everything into mud.

The tongue licked her ear.

Sapphire pried one eye open and glared at her dragon. "Stop that."

Lotus somehow managed to look abashed.

"Come." Karis reached out a hand and what looked like a fairly clean rag. "Wipe your face off so you don't scare the entire village, and then let's go get you all some dinner. Things will look far more cheerful in the morning, I promise."

Sapphire had her doubts, but she let the older woman pull her to her feet.

Karis cast a glance at Afran. "Maybe you can fly on ahead and let Inga know to expect us." She winked at the girl on his back. "Go the long way."

Sapphire sighed as the two of them lifted into the sky in perfect dragon flight.

She and Lotus were doomed. Just doomed.

Chapter 10

Sapphire bit into her second meat pie, humming with pleasure as the warm juices ran out onto her tongue. This was so much better than dust, even if Inga had screeched and made her go wash up at the pump a second time before she'd let her in the kitchen to collect her dinner tray.

The meat pies were worth the second scrubbing in cold water. They were flaky and buttery and full of stewed venison so soft, it melted on her tongue almost as fast as the pastry.

Kellan was making her way steadily through a second pie as well. Karis, eating more slowly, watched the two of them in amusement. Sapphire downed half a mug of honey wine and took another bite of her pie. There were fruit tarts for dessert, but she wasn't ready to switch to the lighter fare yet.

Maybe if she ate enough, she'd be too heavy for Lotus to carry her tomorrow.

Karis reached for a tart and chuckled. "Eat up. You'll want your strength for the morning."

Sapphire groaned. "I'm going to bed and not getting up for a week."

Kellan snorted. "I'm not cleaning your chamber pot for that long, so you'll have to come up with some other way to hide."

Said the elf whose dragon hadn't planted her in the dirt even once.

She wasn't planning on hiding, exactly. She just intended to stay firmly attached to the ground. "Maybe Lotus needs more flying lessons without me first so she can practice those new wing angles." A moment of inspiration struck. "Maybe she could carry a bag of rocks on her back." Something that wouldn't break quite as easily as an elf.

"Rocks don't have brains," Karis said crisply. "It's your job to help Lotus think while she's in the air, and a bag of rocks or straw or whatever else you were going to suggest isn't going to be able to do that."

Kellan grinned. "Maybe a sack of meat pies. Tell Lotus she can eat all the ones she doesn't dump in the dirt by the end of the lesson."

Sapphire stared at her friend and nearly handed over all her fruit tarts in gratitude. "You're a genius."

Karis shook her head, nixing that idea quickly. "Lotus cares at least as much about you as she does about meat pies. The problem isn't her motivation, unlike some other students I can name. You just need more practice."

Why were teachers always so fond of that line? "I think we might be hopeless."

"It went well for a first lesson," Kellan said staunchly.

Sapphire snorted. "I bet there hasn't been a worse first lesson in the history of dragonkind."

They both turned to look at Karis, whose lips twitched. "Don't ask me, younglings. I'm not *that* old."

Kellan grinned. "Afran is."

Judging from the snores, Afran was fast asleep. Sapphire looked at the much smaller peach-pink lump curled up beside him. Lotus hadn't even managed to finish half a meat pie before she'd fallen over beside the much larger dragon, sound asleep.

"Don't worry," Karis said affectionately. "She'll be fine in the morning. She's young and strong and healthy — the only part of her that's truly tired is her brain."

That was pretty much the only part of Sapphire that felt like it was still working. "Why do we have to learn to fly, anyhow?" She knew she was whining, but she couldn't find enough self-control to stop. "We could find a job that doesn't need us to fly. Like helping Irin and Kis in the nursery."

Kellan snorted. "Lotus would rile up the babies all day long with her antics, and Kis would probably set both of you on fire before sundown."

Probably. But Irin loved Lotus, even when she was a total troublemaker. Sapphire sighed and looked over at their silent teacher. "I'm guessing we don't get to quit after our first lesson."

Karis's smile was slight, but there was approval in her eyes. "You guess rightly. If the two of you truly can't figure out how to fly together, we'll find a way for you to make your contribution to the world from the ground. But that would be a decision made many lessons down the road. You need to fight your way through the learning first, just like Alonia doesn't get to give up on languages or Lily on cooking or Kellan here on holding her own in a fight."

Kellan was even tinier than Sapphire, and she took a bruising every time they went for weapons training. Which meant the next part of the answer was the same one Irin always gave to Kellan when she picked herself out of the dirt and glared at him. "You want us to be as prepared as we can be when we leave the village."

"Indeed." Karis looked down into her mug for a long moment. "We do that for all of our students and young dragons, but with you and Lotus, it goes beyond the usual need to prepare. Elhen bade us get you ready, and that's a responsibility Afran in particular takes very seriously."

She hadn't known that — but she knew why. Something lurched inside Sapphire's chest. She never liked thinking about this part. "Because we're one of the five." Two years ago, that had felt wonderfully special. These days, it just felt like a blacksmith's anvil waiting to fall on their heads. She knew how many dragons and kin never came back from their tours, and they were the ones out on the ordinary kinds of assignments.

She and Lotus had been picked for something far scarier. If the old stories were true, they were part of a very small, very special group that would save all of dragonkind. Something Sapphire mostly managed not to think about because it just made her teeth chatter. "I don't even know what that means, or what we're supposed to do." They were just one small dragon and one bruised elf. Maybe the Dragon Star made a mistake.

Karis's hand on her shoulder was gentle. "We

assume you were chosen for a reason, and that in the fullness of time, we'll know what it is that you're meant to do. In the meantime, we'll prepare you like every other youngling of this village so that you're as ready to face life as we can possibly make you. Which means nourishing both your strengths and your weaknesses."

Sapphire wanted to have a temper tantrum just thinking about more bruises, because she knew exactly what their weakness was—but something Karis had said stopped her. Her body felt thoroughly abused, but she was pretty sure she didn't have any more dings than Kellan had after a hard weapons lesson—and her best friend never complained. She just stood up, dusted herself off, made a face at Irin, and attacked him again.

Not once in the two years Sapphire had been here had it ever worked. Irin always plunked her right back in the dust, and he never did it gently. But it never stopped Kellan from trying. Sapphire looked over at her best friend, seeing her in a new light. "One of your strengths is that you never stop trying, no matter what happens."

Kellan flushed, embarrassed by the praise. "I'm just stubborn. That's all."

"It's far more than that." Karis emptied the last of her cup. "You've got a deep and steady faith, and you hold on to it when others might give up."

Kellan sat wordless, her cheeks bright pink.

"That will be needed," Karis said quietly. "The dragons are depending on us to save them, and they will need all our strengths. Not just those of the five."

Sapphire swallowed hard. Two years ago, Elhen's tale had been a pretty story about saving the dragons of old — until one night in the dark about a week later when she'd realized that if the ancient dragons perished, there wouldn't be any dragons in the here and now, either. No Afran, no Kis, no Elhen — and definitely no peach-pink, barrel-rolling, bed-stealing most amazing dragon in all the world.

Life without Lotus wasn't something she even wanted to think about. Sapphire reached out to her best friend and took her small, sturdy hand. "I need you to teach me how to be as tough as you are when Irin beats you up with a sword."

Kellan flashed a grin. "I can teach you all the swear words I say in my head. Those help the most."

Sapphire bit back a snort and glanced at Karis.

Karis raised a wry eyebrow. "Once Kellan runs out of curses, come see me." She winked at Kellan. "The weapons master before Irin wasn't any friendlier, and I wasn't much bigger than you are."

Nobody who rode on Afran's back had any need for a sword, but swear words might be useful for all kinds of reasons. Lily knew some pretty good ones from hanging around the docks in the fishing village where she'd been born. And Alonia knew how to say things so politely that people didn't even realize they'd been cursed.

None of that would help Sapphire and Lotus fly any better, but it did help move the scary anvil a little farther away from her head. She might be one of the five, but she had a lot of friends at her back.

Which was as good a reason as any to get up tomorrow and go drown in some more dust.

Chapter 11

Sapphire groaned as she walked out the door of the small rondo she shared with Kellan and headed toward the nursery. Everyone kept telling her that flying would hurt less with practice, but it had been almost two weeks now, hours every day, and getting out of her bed each morning was still the hardest part of her day.

Which was saying something because it had plenty of competition. Lotus had mastered her wing tilts and tail curls well enough to keep them out of accidental nose dives, but the crashes due to lack of thought on the part of a certain peach-pink dragon's immature brain were still happening frequently enough that Sapphire's whole body had turned into one big bruise.

Hopefully, whatever Irin wanted her for

would be quick and easy and very soft.

He looked up as she ducked inside the dim nursery. "Good morning."

She'd take his word for it. "I got a message that you wanted to see me." It wasn't an unusual request — Lotus still spent a lot of time with Irin and Kis, and there was a never-ending list of chores associated with raising baby dragons, including the oversized ones.

Irin grunted. "I'll be doing your flying lesson this morning."

She blinked — that was pretty much the last thing she'd expected. Kis had been wing-wounded many seasons past and didn't fly any farther than the nearest sunning rock.

"You think I've forgotten all I know just because we don't take to the skies anymore, missy?" Irin's voice was testier than usual. "I'll have you know that in our day, there wasn't any dragon who could outfly Kis, and not a rider who could stick like I could, either."

Things were starting to make a bit more sense. "You can teach me not to fall off?"

"I can try." He raised a wry eyebrow. "Afran tells me that teaching Lotus to be more thoughtful about which way she's pointing her feet hasn't been all that successful."

Sapphire sighed. "She barrel-rolled me again yesterday." Barrel *smash* was more like it. "I managed to hang on long enough to hit the ground feet first, but I'm not sure that's a big improvement." Her hips ached like demons this morning.

"Not if you're any higher up than the rooftops, anyhow." Irin clapped a hand on her shoulder. "Come. I sent Lotus out to practice earlier. Let's go see what she's learned."

She didn't need a dragon with more tricks. Sapphire limped along after Irin as he stomped out the nursery door and headed out the back way to the north edge of the village. That worried her — the land was a lot rockier up there. "We've been practicing in the south fields."

"Too flat for what we need."

She suddenly felt positively nostalgic about the clouds of dust. "I'm not sure I'm ready for anything else."

Irin turned to her, his eyes flashing fiercely. "Life doesn't always wait for you to be ready, missy. It's time to practice somewhere that doesn't offer you and that girl of yours a soft landing. Get both of you paying better attention to the job you need to do."

He stomped off and she followed his back, abashed, looking at the hunched set of his shoulders. However harsh his words might have been, he'd paid a steep price to learn them. One she hadn't thought about very much, and that suddenly shamed her. He probably hadn't felt ready to fly into an oncoming army with no backup either—but she was very certain he wouldn't want to talk about that. So she asked the other question that was making her feel guilty and sad. "Do you miss flying?"

His shoulders hunched a little further. "Like I'd miss my right arm, but Kis can't manage the wing tilts anymore, and we'd be a sad ghost of what we used to be even if we managed it."

Which would embarrass the old, proud dragon even more than it would his rider. Sapphire tried to imagine Kis's rich gold wings flapping in the sunlight. "I wish I'd seen you."

"Ah, we were a sight, we were." Irin looked up at the sky, smiling. "Kis could dive from the sky like a hawk and pull up so close to the grass, I could have picked myself a four-leaf clover."

That sounded like something she wanted to try exactly never. "Did you ever fall off?"

The silence stretched for long enough that Sapphire thought it might never break. Finally, Irin sighed. "Only once. The day Kis got hurt."

And he'd never gotten back on. Her heart ached for him and his dragon both.

"Come." Irin turned left on a small trail leading to a rocky outcropping.

Sapphire's legs groaned in protest, but she didn't have time to listen to them. She was far too busy looking at a peach-pink dragon perched on the top of a boulder almost as high as her head.

Irin's hand stretched out to stop her. "She hasn't seen us yet. Watch."

Lotus tiptoed up to the edge of the boulder, wings curled around her protectively, tail stretched out behind for ballast. Then she spread her wings, puffed smoke out both nostrils, and jumped.

Sapphire held her breath as Lotus caught a small updraft and glided several feet, wings barely moving, before she dropped to the ground light as a cat. "Oh. That was beautiful." Graceful and elegant and a lot of things she'd never associated with Lotus in flight before.

"She's doing well." Irin's words were brisk, but his eyes held something different. "She's still a young one. People would do well not to forget that."

Sapphire hoped he remembered that *she* was still young too—and would very much like to live to see her next birthing day.

"Let's get you on, then." Irin was moving again, headed for the small boulder.

"I'm going to ride her while she does that?" That seemed like a really bad idea. Sapphire remembered the nose dives in the field all too well.

"You are." He scrambled up the last pitch of scree and reached up and gave Lotus a pat on the shoulder. "Climb on up now, and I'll show you a couple of tricks to help you stay on her when she does the unexpected."

Unless he had a pot of tar to glue her down, Sapphire was pretty sure there wasn't anything that was going to keep her from meeting up with a boulder head first. She clambered up, thinking she probably should have just jumped out of the tree back when Lotus had first hatched and been done with it. This way of dying came with way too many broken bones.

"Not there." Irin's hands pulled her toes from the spot where Karis had told her to put them. "That works fine with nice sedate dragons who mostly fly on diplomatic missions, but it's a damn fool way to ride a dragon who might fly upside down."

Sapphire couldn't argue with that.

"Bend your knees and tuck your heels in right here." He was positioning her feet back under Lotus's wings, in tight to her body. "Feel that ridge there? Find a good solid place to tuck your toes along that."

It felt totally weird, and from the way Lotus was squirming, it was also ticklish. But Sapphire finally got one foot situated, and then she understood what Irin was trying to get her to do. In between the wing bones and the flexible skin that attached to Lotus's back, there was almost a pocket. One that surrounded her foot and held it tight and steady.

"Just like that." Irin scratched under Lotus's chin and sounded pleased. "Now stand up a little — get your weight off her back."

Sapphire was astonished to find that she could do so with ease.

Irin nodded his approval. "Good. Now try hanging off to the side."

She eyed him like he might be crazy, but did as she was told. The foot pockets were surprisingly helpful — she could push against them from any angle, or flex her feet up to hold herself against the forces of gravity trying to pull her off sideways.

"Just like that. Once your feet get strong, you'll be able to hang on like that for hours, even if this silly girl decides to roll herself upside down."

Everything in her wanted to deny that was possible, but she could feel the beginnings of the truth of what he said in her own feet. They were warm and anchored and secure, and it didn't take nearly as much effort as the other ways she'd been trying to stay on. "I think this will help. Thank you."

"You're light. That makes this easy." He patted Lotus on the shoulder. "Back up on the rocks, missy. Same exercise, but with your rider this time." He looked up at Sapphire as she reached for the neck spines. "No hands. You hold on with your feet. You never know what you might need those hands for someday."

She stared at him. "You want me to jump off a rock and not hold on?"

His grin was the scariest thing she'd seen all morning. "No. I want Lotus to jump off a rock. You're just the passenger." He tossed her an apple from his pocket. "I don't want you to take any bites from this unless you're in the air. You can stop your lesson for the day once the apple is gone or when the sun sets, whichever comes first."

The cool, firm skin of the apple in her hands felt like her last slim hold on reality. "I'm going to fall off long before that."

He shrugged his shoulders. "Then your apple will be dirty and your head will hurt from whatever rock you banged it into, and you'll get back on and try again."

Words fired up in her throat. Angry ones. Scared ones.

He leaned in, his head at the level of her knee, his eyes locked on hers. "I would give both my legs and every other body part I could spare to get to do this even one more time. Stop thinking about what you're scared to do and start remembering that you're dragon kin and your dragon is healthy and young and capable of dancing in the sky, and that's a rare privilege."

Sapphire gulped. His eyes looked a bit like Kellan's. Full of yearning.

She tucked her feet a little deeper under Lotus's wings. "Okay. Let's go fly off some rocks."

Irin nodded and turned to go.

She stared at him. "Aren't you going to stay and watch?" Someone had to pick up the pieces when she broke.

He shook his head without turning back. "This is something the two of you need to do."

She heard the words he didn't say. It would hurt him too much to stay.

Chapter 12

Sapphire plunked down on a tuft of moss at the edge of the river. There were flat sunning rocks nearby, but she didn't want to so much as touch a rock ever again. Her head had more than one fist-sized lump, courtesy of some boulder that didn't have the decency to get out of the way of her wild tumbles. One of her ears bore a dent that was probably permanent, and the rest of her body looked like it had fought with an avalanche and lost.

She looked over at Lotus, who had flopped down in a patch of sun and laid her head morosely on a fallen tree trunk. Her dragon wasn't in any better shape than she was. "We're a sorry pair, aren't we, girl?"

Lotus managed a feeble chirrup. Her scales

didn't bash and dent as easily as elf skin, but her normal ebullient confidence had taken some very hard hits. They'd managed a few short flights off a couple of boulders, which was more than they'd ever accomplished in the south field, but the landings had not been pretty. And that was the best of what they'd managed to do. The rest of the rock-and-roll day didn't bear thinking about.

At least there hadn't been anyone watching. They'd always had an audience while they'd practiced in the fields, and even Kellan's hopeful encouragement had gotten heavy after a while. It had been easier to dent and bruise alone.

Guilt had kept her at it for a while, and then sheer determination to outlast a bunch of rocks, which wasn't going to win her any smart-elf awards. The last couple of times, she'd dragged herself up onto the boulder fueled solely by the desire to knock herself unconscious for a week.

That would probably excuse them from flying practice.

Sapphire reached into her rucksack, which she'd wisely stowed well away from their practice boulder, and pulled out a fruit tart that was only a little mushed. "Here, I saved this for you. You fell asleep before you got to eat yours last night." It was in far better shape than the apple that had tumbled out of her hands so many times it had eventually turned into sauce. Irin might think holding on was optional, but Sapphire was wildly unconvinced.

Not that two hands had kept her attached to her dragon, either.

A long pink tongue reached out and slurped up the treat, and this time, when Lotus laid her head back down on the fallen tree, her mood didn't feel quite so morose.

Sapphire wished the rest of what ailed them could be fixed with something as simple as a sweet treat. However, she was done worrying about that for the day. They'd come here to recover, not to dig themselves deeper into the pits of despair. She looked over at the small pool of water separated from the river by a painstakingly built stone wall. Sometimes rocks could be useful. "Do you have enough energy left to heat up the water, beautiful?"

Lotus puffed smoke out her nose.

Sapphire grinned — that was probably intended more as a commentary on the foolishness of getting wet than it was on her dragon's firepower. Lotus, like every other dragon in the village, looked highly askance at the strange desire of humans and elves to immerse themselves in water, but they all willingly took turns heating up the small pool that had been built under Lily's direction.

Sapphire had helped move small rocks for two days, highly skeptical of Lily's plan — until Afran had streamed fire into the water for the first time and they'd all climbed into the steaming, blissfully warm waters. That first soak had converted even the most skeptical, and the river had become a frequent stopping place for most of the village after that. It was the best cure ever for winter chills, lonely hearts, and bruised-and-battered bodies.

Lily came every day, rain or shine, and Alonia manufactured herself plenty of heart troubles deserving of a visit, but Kellan and Sapphire prized the pool most for its ability to cure their physical aches and pains. Which meant it was high time she got in. She slid out of all but her light underlayer and glanced at her dragon.

Lotus ambled over and sniffed at the surface of the pool, checking for whatever hobgoblins the dragons thought lived in the waters, and then blew a delicate, careful stream of fire into the middle. She stopped as soon as the water started to steam — they'd learned through trial and error and the curses of the occasional elf foolish enough to stay in during reheating that even a small dragon could raise the water temperatures far past what was comfortable for the pool's occupants.

Sapphire scratched behind Lotus's ears in thanks. Dragons were useful for so many things.

She dipped her toes in the water, feeling a little guilty. She should have invited Kellan. Warming the waters just for one was a spoiled-elf indulgence, especially when there were always others who would welcome the chance for a soak — and Kellan would be mourning the loss of her daily ride on Afran.

Sapphire kicked her toes, causing ripples in the water. Truth be told, she hadn't wanted the company. Irin was right — they needed to walk this alone, she and Lotus and the fear that lived between them. Maybe if they tumbled down the rocks often enough, the fear would crack open and melt away.

The fear — and the shame.

Sapphire dipped her legs farther into the warm water and leaned her head over on Lotus's neck. "We'll figure it out, girl. One day, we'll be the best fliers in the village." She wished her heart felt more certain. Dragons were born to fly. Everyone said so, but they'd said that Moon Clan daughters were born to be special too, and no amount of effort had ever made Sapphire into anything more than an absolutely ordinary elf.

::Don't underestimate what lies within you, youngling. The star has marked you for a reason.::

The voice from behind had Sapphire spinning her head around in shock. That was two dragons in a month that had deigned to talk to her. When she saw who had spoken, she yanked her feet out of the water and tried to assemble herself into some sort of position of respect, Lotus quivering at her side. The queen's guardians rarely came down to the village, and when they did, they never seemed to notice mere younglings. "Ciara. We are honored."

The silver-gray dragon nodded her head regally. ::You have been working hard on your flying. Elhen wishes you to know that she has observed your progress and finds herself proud of both dragon and kin.::

They'd had an audience after all. Sapphire didn't ask how the queen had seen — she had ways and means far beyond those of mere mortals. Honesty turned Sapphire's cheeks bright pink as she admitted to what the dragon in front of her almost certainly already knew. "We're mostly still just falling."

The guardian turned her gaze on a trembling Lotus. ::No dragon should ever be ashamed of falling down. The greatest hearts are forged in the fires needed to get back up. Elhen is not yet certain if you will ever manage to fly the skies together, but she sees much progress in the forging of your hearts.::

Sapphire could feel the overwhelmed awe streaming from Lotus, and slid a little closer to her dragon as surreptitiously as she could. "Please convey our deep thanks to the queen." She tried to think of what else to add, but it would be grievously impolite to ask Elhen to stop watching their failures, and her brain had hit far too many rocks to come up

with any other words appropriate for the ears of a
dragon queen.

Ciara's eyes held a momentary twinkle as if
they'd heard Sapphire's unspoken thoughts, and
then she reached out an elegant claw and set a small
pot on the rocks next to them. ::This is a salve the
queen uses on her own aching joints. She bade me
tell you to soak in the foolish waters if you must,
but to use this after. It will help your bruises heal
by morning.::

Sapphire managed not to groan. If Elhen
expected them to be flying again tomorrow, there
was no hope that Karis or Irin might be convinced
to grant them a reprieve. She lifted the lid off the
small container and tried not to wince at the smell
that wafted out. Dragon balms had renowned
healing qualities, but they generally smelled like
something three days dead. This one was no
exception. "Please thank the queen for such a
generous gift." Lotus was eyeing the jar with
interest, and that was plenty of reason to be
grateful.

Ciara nodded one last time and then spread
her wings, looking straight at the young dragon. ::I
will see you in the skies.::

It was the traditional dragon farewell.

It wasn't the guardian's fault that it stabbed at
both of their hearts.

Chapter 13

It took two weeks. Two weeks of solitary work from morning to dark up in the boulders north of the village. But the day finally came, and Sapphire marched through the village and into the nursery and straight over to the man who had taught her that sometimes you have to do things the hardest way possible, and held out an apple core.

He glanced down at it.

She could feel the pride in every line of her body — for her, and for Lotus, and for what they had done together. "I took the last small nibble during a barrel roll on the way home." One that had made her teeth clatter, but she'd done it. It was the first day they'd been anywhere close to the milestone that let them quit before sunset, and every bruise on her body had insisted that she get the job done.

Irin reached out and took the core and juggled it on his palm. "Took you a while."

It had. And the man who had abandoned them to the rocks on the first day had never come back, not even once, but today she didn't care about that. "We needed some practice." It had been the hardest work of her life, and the proudest. The look in Lotus's eyes when they'd landed after the barrel roll, smooth as silk, had been worth every hard minute.

A tiny green dragonet scampered up Irin's pant leg and sniffed the apple core. He scratched the top of its head. "Be careful, little one. There's courage in this apple."

Sapphire laughed — she couldn't help it. "Not hardly. I might be the least brave person ever to ride a dragon."

"Don't be foolish." Irin held still as the baby dragon crunched the treat in his hand. "Courage is being afraid and doing the damn thing anyhow."

She thought about that, and it lit a quiet glow somewhere deep in her belly.

He settled the baby dragon on his shoulder and then looked her in the eye. "You know what you need to work on next."

She cringed inside, both at his relentless tone and at the knowledge that she did indeed know.

They'd tried, a little at least. Anything more than ten feet off the ground gave her and Lotus both hives. "I don't know if we're ever going to be able to go high." There was such a huge difference between jumping off a boulder and falling out of the sky.

Irin thumped a hand on her shoulder that was probably meant to be comforting. "That's a worry for another day. On this one, take the rest you've earned."

Lotus was already happily following that plan. She'd buzzed the far edge of the village in tired jubilation and then headed straight for the sunning rocks where the other dragons congregated in the late afternoon. "I should probably go find Kellan and see if I can help with supper." Flying practice had displaced most of Sapphire's usual contributions to village life, and her best friend had been picking up the slack.

"That's a fine thought." Irin's voice sounded gruffer than usual. "The two of you are good for each other. Go help with dinner, and then take yourselves off and do whatever it is young girls do for fun."

Sapphire tried not to giggle — generally that meant playing a joke on one of the village elders, and Irin was one of their favorite choices.

The gleam in his eye said he knew that — and

that he knew all too well which way her thoughts had turned. "There have been fewer pranks around here lately, what with you and Kellan so busy."

They'd have to fix that. Kellan was the best at teasing Kis out of his ill tempers, but they could all do it in a pinch. It was an unspoken pact in the village that the dragon with the hole in his wing would never be left to stew too long in his old and cranky juices.

Irin set the green dragonet on the floor. "You'll do well to stay away from here tonight. Kis is feeling particularly stiff, and he's likely to singe the hair off any youngling foolish enough to bother him."

They'd have to see about that, but she was sorry the old dragon was hurting. Sapphire thought about the magic salve and reached for her rucksack. "Ciara gave us a pot of balm that might help him. We used some of it, but there's still lots left." Lotus had very much enjoyed its benefits, but Sapphire hadn't been able to tolerate the smell. The only thing worse than being beat up by rocks was smelling like you'd let the goats poop on you afterwards.

Irin took the lid off the salve and raised an eyebrow. "This is the one Darius flies in from the borderlands. Some old hermit up there makes it each winter. It's costly stuff, but if it helps Kis, I'll work out a way to trade for some."

All the more reason not to use it on a few bumps and bruises that would heal on their own. "You can keep the pot. Lotus can come by if she needs to use a little."

Irin looked amused. "Offended by the smell of it, are you?"

Sapphire felt her cheeks go pink. The nursery master teased them unmercifully about such foolish attitudes during weapons training. "I like to go have a soak instead, and Kellan made me a tea balm." Which might not work quite as well, but it smelled oceans better.

"Kellan's got a fair hand with salves."

The giddiness of a successful flight tickled Sapphire's ribs and prompted her to say exactly what she was thinking. "She should have — you give her enough bruises to practice on."

Irin's laughter, loud and booming, sounded raspy, like he hadn't used it in a long time. The green dragonet scurried under a low table and watched him with wide eyes.

Sapphire grinned at the baby. The hatchlings learned soon enough that Irin's bark was far worse than his bite, but apparently this one had never heard him laugh. No surprise there — it was a rare enough thing. She eyed the older man carefully, wondering if he'd always been that way.

Or whether falling out of the sky had changed him.

He turned, smoothing out an invisible wrinkle in the weaving that covered his work table. "If you've got a question, ask it."

She did — she just wasn't sure where to begin. "What was it like for you and Kis? After he got injured?" Everyone knew the story of how the brave dragon had attacked from the sky, over and over, Irin on his back, as they single-handedly tried to stop an advancing army. It was the day that had made them heroes, but people rarely talked about what happened after.

Sapphire had heard a few things. About the honor guard of dragons that had flown them back to the village on a huge sailcloth as soon as Kis was stable enough to be lifted. About the man who hadn't left his dragon's side for three moons.

"There are those who will tell you we were brave." Irin started taking small pots and jars out of the wooden box that served as his medicine chest, arranging them carefully on his table. "They'd be lying. We were cranky and angry and as out of sorts as man and dragon can be."

Sapphire held her breath, amazed that he was answering her question.

"Kis was in great pain, so I would lean against him deep into the night and tell him tales of battle and victory and all the injuries we'd survived to fight again. I spun the hope that we would make it through the dark and the pain and take to the skies again, just like we'd always done."

She could hear his bone-deep, shattered sadness. "Did you ever try to fly again?"

"We did. All the healers who came told us not to, but we tried anyhow. I took Kis to the same rocks where you've been practicing."

Sapphire winced. No wonder he hadn't stayed that first day.

"We climbed to the top of the highest boulder, and I told him to stretch his wings and go meet the sky." Irin glanced over at the sleeping Kis and waited for his next snore. "He made it about the span of a planting field and then crumpled to the ground."

Sapphire's heart broke for the proud man and his dragon. "That must have been terrible."

"Terrible was still to come." Irin moved a small purple bottle, and his hands were shaking. "Every morning, we walked out to the rocks. Some days, Kis could fly a little farther. Two fields, or even three. Some days, he couldn't even lift off the rock."

She had some small idea of what that was like—trying day in and day out, with so very little to show for all the effort.

"It took us an entire summer to give up. Kis knew the truth first. My head was far harder. I was arrogant, and I pushed him far past what I should have."

Sapphire wanted badly to give the old warrior a hug, but she knew he would never stand for it. "Do you fly with anyone else?" It wasn't something she'd ever heard of, but if Afran could give Kellan a ride, anything was possible.

"No." Irin took a long look at the sleeping dragon in the corner. "It would break his heart. And mine."

The bond of kin. Sapphire squared her shoulders. Her dragon had young, strong, healthy wings. "We'll keep trying."

Irin's shoulders hunched over his pots, and he suddenly looked tired and old. "Go," he said gruffly. "Smart warriors know to rest between the battles, to enjoy a bit of the life they're fighting for. Kis and I never did enough of that."

Sapphire walked slowly out of the rondo, thinking about Irin's words and his sadness, his rusty laugh and the pride in his eyes when she'd walked in with her mostly eaten apple. Out on the rocks alone with Lotus, day after day, getting bruised and battered and worn, it was easy to forget all the reasons why they bothered. Irin had just reminded her of one more.

He'd also reminded her that there was more to life than flying and failing. She looked around and saw a dark head and a blonde one, tilted together in a pose that said there was trouble brewing. Perfect.

Lily looked up as she approached. "Hey, look who's decided to grace us with her presence."

Sapphire stuck out her tongue. "I got tired of leaving my skin all over a bunch of rocks, so I decided to take a break."

Alonia looked concerned. "How's it going?"

It was nice to have good news to share for a change. "I had enough time to eat a whole apple today." Her friends knew of Irin's challenge. She only got to eat the apple while airborne. "It was a really small one, though."

A big smile bloomed on Alonia's face. "The size doesn't matter."

Lily snorted. "That's not what you say about your bottom."

Their flirtatious friend patted her ample curves and grinned. "You just wish you weren't all bony and cranky and sour-faced."

Sapphire hid a grin. Life, entirely back to normal. "Apparently, the two of you haven't been keeping up our reputation. Irin says the pranks have been too quiet lately."

Lily raised a skeptical eyebrow. "He said no such thing."

"He did." More or less, especially if you were an elf who was good at reading between the lines. "He said to stay away from Kis or we'd get our hair flamed." Which sounded like an invitation and a dare all rolled into one.

"Oh, did he, now?" Lily looked intrigued.

Good. Kellan might be the most fun-loving of the four of them, but Lily had the most devilish ideas—and Alonia could always convince anyone they might need to help them. "Let's go rescue Kellan from the kitchens and see if we can shake things up a little around here. Maybe Inga will help." Or at least give them a bit of roast venison. The cranky woman who ran the kitchen had a soft spot for Kis.

Alonia shook her head and hooked elbows with the two of them. "Inga? Are you sure you didn't hit your head on a rock a little too hard?"

Every single day for the last two weeks, but she couldn't let that stop her. It was time to celebrate—even Irin said so.

Although he might change his mind by the end of the night.

Chapter 14

It was cold, and they were so impossibly high. Sapphire closed her eyes and wrapped her fingers tighter around the branch. They would never get out of this tree. They would freeze, and the tiny baby dragon she had promised to keep safe would die.

A touch of warmth brushed her mind.

Lotus.

Sapphire gulped and opened her eyes. It wasn't the tree she clutched tightly, and there was no baby dragon clinging to her chest. She looked down at muscles rippling under peach-pink scales and felt the cold night blasting against her cheeks.

They were flying.

That wasn't possible. Lotus wasn't this big, and she should be able to see something around them besides this terrible, inky, ominous dark. Stars, or maybe the light of a fire from somewhere far below.

She shuddered. She didn't want to think of down.

She reached her mind out to her dragon and felt determination and power — and fear. And in both of their minds, their first linked memory. The tree, impossibly high, swaying in a night almost as dark as this one.

Sapphire's legs ached from holding tight to the rippling muscles as Lotus flapped her wings. She was so tired. So cold. She took a breath, trying to find the fortitude to hold on longer, to stay with this wild flight through the inky black.

Then the evil blackness reached out and knocked them both out of the ominous, unreal sky.

They fell, hurtling down, tumbling into something far worse than a barrel roll, far less controlled. Sapphire closed her eyes and screamed, clutching Lotus with her knees and hands and knowing it would never be enough. There was no soft ground to catch them this time, no big claws to break their fall or kind faces to dust them off.

She could feel the teeth coming for them in the dark, tearing cold, and the wild fear of a young dragon who had tried her hardest and knew it wasn't enough.

They were going to die.

"Sapphire! You need to wake up!"

The hissing voice caught them just before they plunged into the black, gaping maw. Sapphire could feel her heart shuddering as they escaped certain death. Saved by a few words she could no longer hear.

"Sapph. You're okay. You're just dreaming."

That was Kellan's voice, and she sounded really scared. Sapphire wondered for one awful moment if the black maw had gotten everyone.

No, that wasn't possible—Kellan wasn't dragon kin. She couldn't go flying in the dark night. The teeth couldn't eat her. She was safe.

Small, strong hands stroked her cheek. "Can you open your eyes?"

Sapphire hadn't been aware they were closed. She scrunched up her face, trying to find the muscles that would pull her eyelids open. It was hard—they were still fighting against the last awful things they had seen in the dark.

Finally, she got one eye squinted open just enough to see the blurry outlines of a hearth fire. Her head felt totally woozy. "Why am I in the kitchen?"

"Because after talking Lily and Alonia into helping you turn Kis's dinner stew purple, you fell asleep in your supper," said Kellan acerbically. "So we figured it was easier to bed you down here than to carry you back to your room."

Purple stew. Followed by onion soup and crusty bread for dinner. Sapphire swallowed down the rising nausea and lifted her head. Clearly, her best friend had slept in the kitchen beside her instead of leaving to sleep in her own very comfortable bed. "Is Lotus okay?"

Kellan's green eyes got a lot more worried. "She should be tucked in with Kis. Want me to go check?"

The cranky old dragon loved Lotus, even if she was more trouble than a herd of wild pigs. And if something had happened to his young charge, Kis would have set off an alarm loud enough to be heard far beyond the village. "No. I'm sure she's fine—I just had a really bad dream."

Kellan nodded as she moved toward the hearth fire. "You were thrashing like someone was trying to kill you, and then you grabbed my arm and held it so tight, I thought I might have to walk around for the rest of my life with your handprints on my skin."

Sapphire winced—she'd had enough dragon

claws wrapped around her arm to have some idea of how that must have felt. "Sorry. That probably hurt like the devil."

Her best friend snorted as she ladled soup into a clay bowl. "Let's just say I'm glad you let go. Want to tell me what the dream was about?"

It was receding now, but the echoes of the black maw still chilled her heart. "Lotus and I were flying really high. I thought we were in the tree at first." Kellan was the only one who knew she still had nightmares about that. "Then I realized I was holding on to Lotus, and the wind was really cold."

She shivered and pulled the light blanket tighter around her shoulders. "I couldn't see stars. Nothing. Just this awful blackness that wanted to eat us." She shuddered, remembering. "We were flying okay for a bit, but then something scared Lotus and we started to fall. Kind of like a barrel roll, only straight down in this big black hole below us. It looked like a mouth. With teeth."

"Ugh." Kellan wrinkled her nose and started slicing off chunks of bread to go with the soup. "That sounds hideous. I'm glad you woke up."

This time. The dream had that horrible feeling of something that wasn't finished yet. And she was still a child of Moon Clan, even if she'd left home long enough ago that some days, she barely remembered her old life. Dreams had meanings —

sometimes important ones.

Kellan laid down the big bread knife, looking worried again. "Maybe you need to stop your flying practice earlier in the day so it doesn't give you nightmares."

That didn't help Sapphire feel better. Flying was supposed to be the best thing dragons and their kin did together, not the biggest disaster. And definitely not the stuff of black dreams that tried to swallow you whole.

Especially flying practice that had finally gone decently well.

Kellan set the clay bowl on Sapphire's lap and laid a fat slice of bread on top. "Here, eat—I don't think you got much of your dinner before you started snoring."

"I don't snore." The standard response was out before Sapphire even realized she'd said it, and it made her feel better. "Irin snores, Afran snores, and Lily snores when she's been up too late. I do not snore."

"Whatever." Kellan's eyes looked a lot happier. "You can believe whatever you want so long as you eat every bite of that soup."

"Yes, Mother." Sapphire dutifully dipped the thickly buttered bread into broth so thick, it was almost a stew. "Did you make this, or Inga?"

"She did." Kellan bit into a slice of bread of her own. "I set the loaves to rising this morning, though."

Inga was getting old, and everyone tried to pitch in where they could, but Kellan was definitely the helper with the most talent for making things that actually tasted good. Sapphire tried to stick with things that weren't any more complicated than carrying wood and washing dishes. "It's really delicious." It was, and suddenly her stomach felt as hollow as the carved-out logs Irin used for dragonet cradles. She scooped in hot soup as fast as she could manage, using bread and spoon both, and felt it warming places inside her that were still cold from the dream.

Kellan just sat with her, companionably munching on bread and saying nothing.

Sapphire wiped the last of the soup out of her bowl with the last of the bread and chewed it slowly. Then she looked over at her best friend and sighed. "I'm really sorry I woke you."

"You're no worse than the babies." Kellan grinned, taking the sting out of her words. "Between Raphia's little ones and the two new dragonets, it doesn't seem like anyone's getting much sleep lately."

Sapphire hoped fiercely that one of the new hatchlings would grow up into Kellan's dragon.

She knew bonding was a strange thing and nobody knew exactly how dragons and kin chose each other, but if anyone deserved to be a part of that, it was the girl who had lived here her whole life and loved each and every dragon with a fierce intensity no one else could match. Kellan never said a word, even when Charis had bonded with a boy barely six seasons old, but Sapphire had heard her crying softly in her bed.

She reached over and brushed the crumbs off her friend's lap and into the empty soup bowl. "Want to sleep here the rest of the night, or go tuck ourselves into our own beds?" Someone would likely arrive early in the morning to tend the hearth fire, and that wasn't going to be quiet.

Kellan smiled. "Our beds will be cold. Let's just sleep here and then I'll make the bread dough in the morning while you keep snoring."

Sapphire snorted as she curled back down into her bedroll. And smiled as she felt her full belly and the warm fire and the quiet breathing of a friend lull her back to sleep.

Interlude

This time when Lovissa startled from a dream, it was with anguish in her veins. And death. The pitching, awful maw as child and dragon fell from the sky.

She shook her head, trying fiercely to land back in her own cave. The darkness here was friendly. Soothing, warming her bones and holding her tight in the quiet winter.

Here, darkness was peace.

She breathed out fire into the night.

The maw was a terrible hell, but it wasn't what had chased her awake. She had caught snippets of flying lessons from the minds of the dreamers. The antics of a small dragon who flew like the tumbling wind, but would not reach for the sky. The eye-popping bravery of the one who climbed on her back, only to tumble off again.

It would be an amusing story, except for two things. These were the first two chosen to save dragonkind — and they spent more time in the dirt than in the air. The future of dragonkind rested on a dragon and an elf child who couldn't get any farther off the ground than the youngest hatchling. They were only one of the five, but still. It put fear in her heart.

But even that, Lovissa might have entrusted to the wisdom of time.

What stabbed cold swords into her belly was the backdrop. The particular dirt the elf child and dragon kept meeting.

Lovissa did not know that dirt.

If the glimpses she had caught spoke true, dragons would live on — but not here. Not in their beloved Veld. In a land with barren hills and huge trees and strange dwellings that looked not at all like a proper cave. In a land where even the stars in the sky were different, if what the elf child remembered from the night of hatching was right.

Lovissa bent her head down, ashamed that her old heart's first wish was that they would not have to leave in her lifetime. Such a loss she did not think she could bear, even if the fires of life willed it. She wanted to know she would become ashes here, just as all the queens who had come before.

She shook herself. That wasn't what she must think about now. The dream had left her with a task. The child and her dragon wearied. They grew tired of fear and failure and the weight hanging heavy on their small shoulders.

Lovissa knew what lived in the maw — she had seen it swallow too many of her warriors.

And the two chosen by the Dragon Star must not quit.

Because whatever their destiny held, they would need to take to the skies to do it. They did not live in the Veld, or anywhere that any dragon in the last hundred years had ever flown. She knew this. She had been the finest scout of her time before she had accepted the mantle of warrior and queen.

She knew this — but Elhen did not. Perhaps the dragon who was queen in this far-off time didn't speak to the ashes. Perhaps she couldn't. The lands of rocks and strange fields of dirt might be too far away.

It made Lovissa's heart almost heavier than she could bear to think of her dragons having to leave the place they had called home since the beginning of time. It was almost unthinkable. But if they must leave, they would need to know where to go.

They would need a path to follow.

For that to happen, Elhen must know that a way was needed. And the elf child and hatchling, first marked of the Dragon Star, must know. So that they kept practicing their flying and did not fall from the sky.

Lovissa snorted smoke again. She had seen too many dragons fall.

She needed to ready her dragons. They must send a message. One that asked for a map — and asked a tiny peach dragon and her rider to keep trying.

She laid her head down on the rock that had long served as her pillow. She must think carefully of how to do this. She did not believe they would have many chances.

* * *

Lovissa pulled herself up on the speaking ledge, royalty in every line. Her dragons needed to see their queen. Hear this from their queen.

There were rumbles from those assembled below. Baraken, back from his scouting mission to the far passes. Snow would keep them safe now for the winter. He stood guard next to Fonia, young Eleret's sister, honoring her grief.

They would miss Eleret's laughing, dancing presence around the fires this winter.

Lovissa felt the weight of all that she was settling across her wing crests. She wanted to tell her dragons that they must not hate the elves, but she couldn't find the words. Not yet, not while their grief was still so fresh. They must conserve their strength, their conviction, for this thing she meant to attempt.

In the winter, around the fires, would be soon enough to speak of the elves.

She drew in a breath and waited for silence to fall. It came almost immediately. "I have had a dream. One of great import, of queen memory. I saw through the eyes of a daughter of my daughters. Saw of hope — and of great need."

A few of the younger dragons reacted. The older and wiser didn't move so much as an eyelid.

She wished deeply that what she brought them was solely a message of hope. Of survival. Of victory. She would give them what she could. "I saw our kindred, wise and proud and owning the skies with their feats of skill and courage."

Dozens of dragon claws, stomping the ground with approval.

She could not tell them about the elves. Not yet. Let them enjoy the idea that their efforts, their sacrifice made a future for dragonkind possible. She knew that one day, they would walk side by side with their enemies. She didn't know how many battles they would need to fight and win first. She was queen — she would not disarm her warriors too early. "We have knowledge that those who will one day come from us need to know. I need your help to send it to them."

Even the youngest dragons were utterly still now. Listening.

Lovissa let the voices of all the queens rise in her throat. "We will call those who will be kin to us." She had chosen those words very carefully. She would not speak of the elves — but perhaps, if they truly loved those with dragon hearts, those elves of a distant time would hear. "We will sing for them, and show them the skies of our time."

It was the best way she could think of to ask for a map. She prayed that the sons and daughters of her daughters had ears to hear.

Slowly, letting the rumble build from deep in her chest, Lovissa began the song that was known by every dragon ever born. It was a song of heartbeats, of tenderness, of warrior spirit, of life and death and all that was and would be.

The Song of the Dragonveld.

Dozens of voices rose to join hers. Some, merely rumbles, some the dancing lightness of their youngest. One or two that would have been bards in a different time. All of them, thinking of those who would come after them. Those who would be.

Lovissa let the song build, let the sounds tremble on the chill night air. And then she tipped her head back to gaze on the night sky and pushed all that she could see into the place inside her soul that had seen the dream.

Bright, beautiful stars spread across the night sky and streamed into the music and into the vision she built for those who would come from her line. From all their *lines. A message so very simple in its meaning, she could scarcely believe it needed to be said.*

::We are here::

PART III:

Stars & Destiny

Chapter 15

Sapphire jerked out of a dream for the second night in a row and cursed. This was getting very tiresome. She scrubbed her eyes and tried to figure out what had woken her up this time. There was no bile rising in her throat, so it couldn't possibly have been anything as scary as the falling dream. But there had been stars. Lots and lots of stars.

And then the insistent demand that she wake up.

She looked over at Kellan's bed and saw her best friend still curled up like a sleeping kitten. Apparently this nocturnal wake-up call had arrived more quietly than the last one.

And it wasn't actually the middle of the night. Dim rays of light made their way in the window slats. Sapphire shimmied to the foot of her bed, blanket still wrapped tightly around her, to peer out the crack in the shutters. There were noises coming from several rondos. A lot of activity for the crack of dawn.

She needed to check on Lotus. Her dragon had started the night tucked in between their beds, but sometime in the dark, she'd gone, headed for the nursery and Kis's large, warm comfort. Irin said most young dragons grew out of that eventually, but Lotus loved her cranky old nursemaid, even if he snored louder than a midwinter drumming festival.

Sapphire shivered as she pulled on her warmest cloak. The mornings were getting colder — winter was coming. She opened the door, wincing as it creaked, and made a note to ask Inga for some oil for the hinges. Kellan took care of that kind of thing too often.

"You too, youngling?" Karis strode up, looking as relaxed and refreshed as if it were the middle of the day.

Sapphire blinked away sleep. There were dragons in the sky, flying in from the direction of caves and cliffs, and if anyone in the village but Kellan was still asleep, they wouldn't be for much longer. "What's going on?"

Karis's hand settled on her shoulder. "You dreamed of stars?"

Sapphire could feel her forehead wrinkling. "Yes."

"So did Afran and all the dragons within speaking distance."

Afran could mind-speak all the way to Elhen's cave. "Everyone?" That was totally bizarre. Sapphire thought back to the dream. It had been pretty, and the Dragon Star had been particularly bright, but that was all she could remember. Nothing scary, no black teeth trying to eat them, no falling out of the sky. Nothing that seemed like it should wake up the entire village.

Irin poked his head out of the nursery as they walked by. "Stars?"

Karis nodded.

The old soldier disappeared back inside, but from the sounds of it, he wasn't staying in there for long. Lotus popped out the door seconds later, eye ridges high and wings quivering.

Sapphire laid a calming hand on her dragon and looked over at Karis. "What's going on?"

"I'm not sure," said the older woman. "But most importantly for right this minute, Elhen has called for us. We go to see the queen."

Sapphire remembered her last visit to the cave of the nearly translucent white dragon. She looked around at all the people and dragons she could see coming out of their rondos. "How will we all fit?" The queen's cave was spacious, but not big enough for this kind of crowd.

"It's not a private audience," Irin said, rejoining them. "We'll go to the rocks." He stopped, and Lotus stopped with him, and together they watched as a big head pushed aside the flap in the side of the nursery rondo's biggest dome.

Sapphire stared—Kis almost never came outside these days, and when he did, it was on a nice afternoon to go sun himself on a rock somewhere. In the cold light of breaking dawn, he looked different. Not so old and tired and sad. Sapphire spoke under her breath, suddenly a little afraid of a dragon she'd seen a thousand times. "He looks really fierce."

Irin chuckled. "Say that louder, missy—you could pay him no finer compliment."

Kis rumbled and pulled the rest of his body out of the rondo. Then he looked at Irin, lifted his head high, and began leading their small procession in the direction of the hills where the queen lived.

This night was getting stranger and stranger. Sapphire leaned in and pitched her voice low enough that hopefully the mighty dragon in front of them wouldn't hear. "Why is Kis coming?"

"Because he smells a fight," said Irin gruffly.

That made no sense. "It was just a dream."

"It wasn't." Karis exchanged a sharp glance with the nursery master. "It was a message, and one with some urgency behind it."

There was dead silence at that, and then several of the people within earshot started nodding their heads and murmuring.

Sapphire stared — all she'd seen were some stars. Nothing that felt this important. "Why would someone send everyone a dream of a bunch of stars?"

"Wrong question." Irin answered her without turning around. "Far more important is who sent it."

That was a creepy thought. Sapphire snugged her cloak tighter around her shoulders and tried not to shiver. She didn't want strangers invading her sleep.

Karis set a hand on Sapphire's shoulder, but it was Irin she answered. "Every dragon we know got the message — and all kin. Only a dragon queen has that kind of power."

Something sharp stabbed in Sapphire's ribs. "That's why Kellan didn't wake up." Or Lily, or Alonia, or any of the other unbonded inhabitants of the village. It was a divide that felt wrong. An odd sort of uneasiness that went all the way down to her bones.

"Elhen would have sent such a message to everyone, those without dragons as well." Irin's voice had a hard edge to it. "This didn't come from her. There were undertones. Whoever sent that message doesn't like elves very much."

Karis nodded. "I felt that too. I'm not sure it was sent to any elves on purpose. Afran says all the dragons heard it, bonded or not. Those of us who are kin might have picked it up by accident."

Sapphire shivered again. Dragon queens rarely bonded, but she had never heard of Elhen showing kin anything but respect. "I don't like this. We should wake everyone." Weird dreams were one thing. A potential enemy was something far different.

Irin eyed her steadily over his shoulder. "We don't know yet what the message means or who sent it. For now, those of us who heard the message will go hear what Elhen has to say. But we won't stand for the exclusion of those who stand fierce and brave at our sides. You have my word on that."

Other heads nodded.

Sapphire let out a breath she hadn't known she'd been holding.

Ciara met them when they were halfway up the steep path to the rocks below Elhen's cave. "She asks for you to assemble. She will emerge and speak with you."

Sapphire gulped. Elhen left her cave even less often than Kis. Whatever this was, it was a very big deal. She stayed quiet as they walked the rest of the way to the rocks. Everyone was solemn and silent — even the dragons landing from the skies seemed to be doing their best to keep their wingbeats hushed.

When they got to the rocks, Sapphire would happily have taken a spot at the back of the gathering, but Kis pushed Lotus forward, and she could hardly leave her dragon standing up front alone. She'd barely taken her position at Lotus's shoulder when the hush grew absolute, every head tilted up to the cliff's edge.

Elhen stood there in the early dawn light, and when she spread her wings, she looked every inch a queen. Sapphire stared as the old dragon flapped once and then glided down to a high rock in front of them all. Her head surveyed them regally, and when her eyes fell on Sapphire and Lotus, they paused for a very long time.

Sapphire's knees started to bang against each other.

"You have all seen the dream. The stars." Elhen waited a beat. "It is a message, sent to us with much power and such urgency as I have never felt before in a vision."

Karis stepped forward. "Afran felt the urgency as well, but not everyone did."

"Of course not." The queen sounded almost amused. "Afran is a dragon of great wisdom, and this was a message of many layers."

Irin growled. "I might not be very wise, but I can tell you that one of those layers isn't very friendly with elves."

"Indeed. Dragons once fought elves." Elhen's voice was resonant, even though her chin barely moved. "The stories say we were once fierce enemies, at war for hundreds upon hundreds of years."

Irin's forehead wrinkled in surprise. "You think this is a message from the dragons way back then?"

"Yes. From their queen." Elhen sounded absolutely certain. "From Lovissa, the great warrior dragon. I can feel her in what I dreamed."

Lotus was squirming, moving from foot to foot, and Sapphire wanted to squirm with her. This all sounded way more complicated than the dream she'd woken up with. Probably because she was just an ordinary elf girl with no wisdom at all—and right now, that sounded like a really good thing, because Lovissa was more than a warrior and queen from some time long past.

She was the dragon who first told the story of the five.

Elhen looked around at the gathered dragons and their kin. "We must speak of this message, for I believe Lovissa would only have sent us a vision of great import. It took much power to do this."

Sapphire stared. It was finally sinking in. She had dreamed a message from a long-dead dragon queen.

Elhen looked up at the dawn sky and the last fading pinpricks of starlight. "This dream was not of our stars. They were the stars of our grandmothers and our grandfathers from a time long past. Our great dragon ancestors, who once fought with the ancestors of our beloved and honored dragon kin."

Sapphire tried to imagine fighting with Lotus and shuddered.

Karis and Afran stepped forward as one, both shaking their heads. "The stars don't change that much. Not even across so many generations."

The old queen's eyes were deep black holes, impossible to read. "I know."

"They might," Irin said quietly. "If they're from far enough back."

Elhen pinned him with a gaze that had Sapphire quaking, and she wasn't even the one it was pointed at. "Are you suggesting that dragons have lost so much of our history? That I do not know precisely how many queens have come before me?"

"No, honored one." Irin's voice was respectful, but firm. "I'm saying that we all got a vision, and sometimes those have meanings that aren't so obvious at first look. We might want to keep our minds open until we take a closer look."

A nervous silence, and then Elhen puffed smoke into the morning air. "That is good advice, old warrior." She raised her head high and looked at everyone gathered. "We have received a message. We do not yet know the fullness of what it means, and we will not act without careful thought and the seeking of dragon and kin and elf and human wisdom on this matter."

A dead silence, and then Afran rumbled again, very quietly.

Elhen nodded regally. "Those who have come before us have sent a message. I believe they are asking for our help—or they believe we need theirs." She paused, and the smoke that came out her nostrils was nearly black. "They are our grandmothers and grandfathers, but these are not our stars. We must know why this is."

She turned her head to Afran. "Find Gilhead and Rhonden. Bring them to me."

The dragons present began a low, scary rumble. Irin looked made of stone. Karis lifted an eyebrow, but said nothing.

Sapphire had no idea what was going on, but she was pretty sure something big and crazy had just taken place.

Kis stepped forward, and Irin beside him. The old dragon snorted fire out his nose. The queen gazed at the two of them for a long time, and then she nodded. "Very well. The two of you will go." She snorted fire of her own at Kis, and her eyes looked almost amused again. "Don't do anything foolish, old man."

Sapphire didn't understand the reply, but whatever it was, it turned Elhen's scales nearly pink.

Chapter 16

Sapphire carried the heavily laden tray of soup and bread and meat pies over to the low table near where everyone was working. Inga and Kellan had the kitchen working overtime producing food for all the star mappers, and anyone who wasn't placing a star or two had been put into service.

She'd stopped trying to help long ago. The dream hadn't felt important, and she'd only been able to remember the Dragon Star with enough accuracy to be useful.

Others had apparently paid far more attention. Enough so that it had taken them the better part of a week to map what had been seen.

She set down the tray and then walked over to the huge flat rock where the mappers were working. The surface of the rock had long ago been blasted by dragons into a sheer surface that was black and shiny and served as a really excellent skating rink in the winter. She and Lotus had spent a lot of cold afternoons running down the hill and then throwing themselves onto the glassy rock and sliding as far as they could.

Today, anyone dragon or elf who tried such a stunt would find themselves on potato-digging duty until they were older than Elhen. The entire flat surface was surrounded by dragons and kin, and every so often, a dragon would lift off and circle in the sky, looking down at all the small white pebbles that were being laid out on its surface.

Sapphire watched as a skinny young kin walked nearly into the center and nudged a stone with his toe and then looked up. "That about right?"

The dragon in the sky over his head rumbled.

Irin nodded on the sidelines. "You've got a good memory, young Joren."

Joren's cheeks turned red. "You taught me to remember the details."

Sapphire grinned ruefully — she'd gotten that speech a whole lot of times too, but clearly it had done Joren some actual good.

The young man who had flown in just before dawn like there were banshees on his heels, yelling that they had the stars in the south of the map wrong, tilted his head. "These definitely aren't our stars. What do you think Queen Lovissa wanted us to know?"

Irin's expression firmed as everyone within ear shot paused what they were doing. "You heard what Elhen told us. Theories wait until we have better knowledge. What we can do right now is to lay out what we know, not what we think."

Joren's face flamed. "Sorry."

Irin's eyes softened a stitch. "Curiosity kills more young lads than sharp swords. Show us what you remember. Gilhead will be finished with his soup soon, and assuming Inga doesn't kill him first, he'll be here wondering why we aren't done with his map yet. Have we fixed the south stones to your satisfaction yet?"

Joren looked at his dragon flying overhead, and then squinted at the scattering of pebbles to his left. "We're close."

"That won't be good enough for Gilhead," Irin said dryly.

Joren's eyes got hard and he muttered something under his breath that Sapphire couldn't hear. It had been that all week, and the mutters had gotten louder when Kis and Irin had returned at the crack of dawn with an exhausted old man and his dragon in tow. Nobody seemed to like their new arrivals. Sapphire hadn't seen the astronomer and his dragon yet, but she'd heard his querulous voice demanding food—and the pot Inga had thrown at his head. She'd been smart enough to scurry away with her tray, but Kellan was trapped in there.

Bad tempers were a regular part of village life, but this level of animosity was something different.

Irin shot a glance at everyone in the vicinity. "If you're not better at mapping than young Joren here, off with you. There's plenty of work to be done, and if you can't find it for yourself, someone will be glad to give you a push in the right direction."

People began to mill about, but Sapphire noticed it was a lot of movement without a whole lot of useful purpose.

Irin just shook his head and looked at the young man standing in the carefully placed pebbles.

"Right. Well." Joren squared his shoulders and nudged a pebble a finger width farther left with his foot. "Something's still not right with this grouping."

Afran rumbled agreement and moved closer to that edge of the star map.

Sapphire handed bowls and meat pies to anyone who wandered near her tray, and tried to keep the sour mess in her belly from rising up her throat. Joren wasn't the only one who wanted to know why the stars were weird. The invisible light of the Dragon Star's mark felt heavy on her forehead. People kept looking at her like they could see it.

She tucked her head between her knees and tried to breathe. Afran had chased all the young dragons away from the mapping rock in no uncertain terms, and she missed Lotus.

Kellan scooted in beside her and gave her a quick, wordless hug.

The nasty feeling in Sapphire's belly settled a little. "What are you doing here?"

"Gilhead's on his way up, and I didn't want to miss it. I can't believe Kis didn't set him on fire."

Sapphire's eyes widened. "Why would he do that?"

"Didn't anyone tell you?" Kellan was whispering, but she sounded shocked. "Back during the big war with the slavers in the south, Gilhead and Rhonden were supposed to be on message relay at the border. They stayed up all night looking at the stars instead and fell asleep on their shift." Her eyes got fierce and sad. "That was the day Irin and Kis signaled that they saw the army coming. Nobody got their message."

Sapphire stared, appalled. She knew the rest

of the story. "So they had to fly into battle themselves. All alone."

Their last flight.

Kellan nodded solemnly. "After the battle, Elhen exiled Gilhead and Rhonden. She said they were a disgrace to dragon and kin and could never come home as long as they lived." She looked over at the rock map, her face uncertain. "Maybe this is their chance to finally do some good."

Or to mess things up for all of dragonkind. "Isn't there anyone else who can help?"

Kellan shook her head slowly. "Elhen never would have sent for them otherwise." She looked over at their weapons master, adjusting a pebble according to Joren's hand signals. "Even Irin thinks so, or he would have run that nasty old man through with his sword."

Sapphire was pretty sure Kis had the better claim. She crossed her arms in front of her chest, angry and uneasy and wishing she could go back in time and kick a sleeping astronomer and his dragon in the knees.

The steady buzz of conversation behind them suddenly hiccupped to a halt. Kellan wiggled sideways to see better. "He's coming," she whispered.

Sapphire hunched down a little smaller.

She watched, rapt, as an old man walked, tapping his cane, over to the high point that gave the best view of the star map. He gazed at it long enough for Sapphire to take three long, quiet breaths, and then glared at the two standing in the middle of the pebbles. "What foolishness is this? Clearly both of you drank far too much last night."

Joren's face turned mottled red, but Irin plunked a restraining hand on his shoulder before the younger man could do anything but splutter. "Neither of us have ever shirked our responsibilities in such a manner, Gilhead. As you can't claim the same, I suggest you start by treating us both with some respect, or I'll be rethinking my position on running you through with my sword."

The old man wheezed. "I was never drunk. Never."

"Which is why you're still alive." Irin's voice was calm and entirely unyielding. "And why you have a chance to be useful. Do you know these stars?"

Gilhead snorted. "No. These are the stars of someone's fevered imaginings."

Irin raised a slow, fierce eyebrow. "You are still kin. You would have seen the dream too."

The old man met the fierce look, but his hands shook with tremors. "I take a sleeping draft. To keep the nightmares away."

Sapphire's hands were shaking too. There was no draft strong enough to take away Kis's pain — or that of the man who loved him. She hated that the ones responsible got to hide from their pain.

Karis stepped forward, Afran at her shoulder. "We know the stars aren't the ones we see. Could the skies have looked like this in Lovissa's time?"

Gilhead snorted again. "No."

Karis only stared at him mildly. "Then how do you explain this star pattern?"

The old man turned to leave. "I don't know, and I don't care. I'm an astronomer, not a storyteller."

Fire hissed from Afran's nose.

Sapphire jumped — Afran was never rude. Ever.

Gilhead turned back, his face an unhealthy shade of red.

"Some of them could be our stars." Joren looked as surprised as anyone at the sound of his own voice. He gulped hard and threaded his way to the far west edge of the map. "This grouping here — that looks like the Wanderer. We see that in our sky, only over in the east. And these over here, if we moved them closer together and took these two out, look like part of the Dancing Ladies."

Sapphire knew how to find the ladies in the sky—but they definitely weren't way over there.

Gilhead looked like he wanted to turn Joren into the next star pebble. "Who are you?"

Irin stepped to the young man's shoulder. "Someone who will get your respect, old man."

The astronomer glared down from his high rock, and then flung his arms at the stars Joren had indicated. "In that case, the answer is obvious. These are the skies as seen from a land far away."

Sapphire froze, as did everyone around her.

Afran stepped forward. ::How far?::

Gilhead shrugged, as if the answer didn't concern him overmuch.

Afran rumbled, his threat abundantly clear.

"Far. At the far reaches of dragon flight or beyond."

The large dragon took a step closer. ::Which way?::

Gilhead glanced at the rocks and flung out an arm again. "If the boy hasn't totally mucked up this map, then a land in that direction."

Sapphire followed his arm—and gulped. Nothing lay that direction. Nothing but ocean.

Water, as far as any dragon had ever flown.

Afran turned to look at his kin and slowly nodded his big head.

A moment later, Karis turned white. And then Irin. And then lazy old Kis stepped up behind his kin and looked as fierce as Sapphire had ever seen him.

All of them looking straight at her.

She could feel her legs trembling. Whatever this was, it was bad. It was scaring the toughest people and dragons she knew—and they all thought it had something to do with her.

Lotus landed beside Sapphire, shaking like an ash leaf, her eyes as big as dinner bowls.

Afran's head dipped, and he puffed gentle smoke in front of Lotus, just like Kis did when a dragonet was fearful. ::You will need to be very brave, my small dragon warrior. You have been chosen for a great task, and now we know some of what will be asked of you.::

Sapphire wrapped her arms around the neck of her dragon and hung on tighter than she ever had. "I don't understand. Someone please tell me what's going on."

It was Irin who stepped forward, and she'd never seen his eyes so gentle. "These are the stars of the dragons of old, missy. The ones you will help save." He paused and took a shaky breath. "Lovissa wanted us to know that this is her sky."

A sky far away. Far out over the waters. Sapphire could barely find enough water in her mouth to speak. "What does that mean?"

He laid a hand on her shoulder. "We don't know. Perhaps the ancient ones had to leave their homeland. All we know for sure is that they are far away."

Far away, far over the waters — and she and Lotus were supposed to help them. She looked into Irin's eyes, begging him to tell her she was wrong. "But we can't fly." Not even over a field, never mind a vast ocean with nothing in it.

He knelt on the ground in front of her and put his hands on her shoulders. "The bravest warriors are the ones who look in the face of the battle they know they might lose — and fight anyhow."

Chapter 17

Sapphire stood in the shadows at the side of her rondo, waiting for a chance to sneak over to the nursery. The village was a flurry of activity, and she didn't want to talk to anyone. The younger dragons had been flying scouting trips over the water, each a little farther than the last. The two that had limped in that morning had been exhausted, but their answer had been the same as the rest.

No land.

And every time such a report came back, people looked at Sapphire and her peach-pink dragon with doubt in their eyes. Worry. Fear.

She didn't even want to think about what that meant. So she would go see the man who always told her to walk one step at a time, because she knew what that next step was and she had no idea how to take it.

She darted out into the sunlight and made it across the path and in through the side door to the nursery without anyone calling her name. She smiled as she stepped inside, into the shadows. Lotus was in the corner, curled up tight against a sleeping Kis.

"She came in the early morning and hasn't woken since." Irin stood at his high bench, weaving sticks into a small nest.

Sapphire walked over and picked up a knife to help whittle off any sharp ends that might poke at tender dragonet scales. "She's been hiding ever since Gilhead's news." She took a breath and looked up at the man who always told her the truth. "Nobody thinks we can do this."

"People are fools," Irin said brusquely. "You are only one of the five, and no one knows what your task will be."

That was exactly what Kellan kept saying, but it wasn't all that comforting. "Everyone thinks we'll need to fly." Out over the water, maybe farther than any dragon had ever flown. To wherever the dragons of old had called home.

"Maybe."

She hung her head. "We've been trying. I

don't know how to get us any farther off the ground."

"She won't until you can." Irin kept weaving twigs. His tough, battle-scarred face wasn't showing any kindness. "Dragons pick up the feelings of their kin, and your scamp is more empathic than most."

Sapphire nodded. "It's strongest when I'm riding her. When we're touching."

"Exactly." He tipped his head at Kis, snoring in the back corner. "I always used to say he could read my mind when I was on his back. Lotus will be picking up your every thought and fear. If you keep remembering that hell-spawned tree she was born in every single moment you're in the air, that's all she'll be thinking about too."

She had more than trees to remember. The black teeth of her dream haunted her too, coming out of the maw and swallowing them both whole. New terrors layered over the old. New reasons to keep their feet firmly on the ground — except they couldn't. Not if Lovissa's stars meant what everyone thought they meant.

Maybe the Dragon Star chose wrong. Or worse. "Maybe I wasn't supposed to be in that tree." Maybe she'd just been an ordinary elf after all, one who got lost at exactly the wrong moment. It was a thought that pierced her with a thousand sharp knives. "Maybe Lotus picked the wrong kin."

Irin's eyes met hers, calm and steady. "No, I don't think she did."

That made Sapphire feel a little better, but she still had no idea what she should do next. Trying to stop the dreams and old fears from haunting her was like trying not to get hungry — it just didn't work. Not any of the ways she'd tried, anyhow.

"You know," Irin spoke casually as he turned toward the small counter where he kept the covered bowl of milk curds. "I grew up near an apple orchard. Loved picking them when I was a boy. If I remember rightly, the best ones were always highest up in the tree."

She stared at him, wondering why in the world the conversation had taken this turn.

And then she thought hard, because Irin never said anything by accident. She thought about two weeks of jumping off rocks and learning to glide. About a dragon who could feel everything she felt. About a man who had once flown with his dragon and didn't get to anymore. About how Kellan's eyes watched Afran when she thought no one was looking, and about just how good a bite of a hard-won apple could taste.

She headed for the door, not even stopping to ask Irin if she'd read his clue right.

She knew what he'd say anyhow. This was her lesson to set, and her lesson to learn.

That sense of confidence stuck with her almost all the way to the apple orchard. She even sang as she walked, a silly summer song Alonia had taught them about maidens with straw in their hair and twinkles in their eyes. The grown-ups always laughed when they sang it, but she didn't care. It felt like the right song to sing as you headed off to pick apples. It carried her all the way to the base of the biggest tree in the orchard, and even far enough to put her hands on the rough bark and look for the first good places to put her feet.

Lotus needed her strong, and being terrified of heights was just foolish if their destiny was to fly the skies together.

Sapphire lifted her foot, clad in a soft boot, to a knobby protrusion just above her knee. She reached over her head and wrapped her arms around a nice sturdy branch, walking her feet a little higher.

This part was fine — it was the thought of what she was going to do next that made her gulp.

She managed to squiggle up to sitting on the first branch and looked down at the ground, trying to breathe calmly. They'd jumped off boulders taller than this and been just fine. She stood up on the branch and reached for another one over her head. This one was skinnier, and it dipped and swayed as she swung her legs up.

It was deeply tempting to close her eyes, but Sapphire knew the whole point of this was to face her fear. She took a seat in a crook close to the tree trunk and looked down. It felt like she saw through two sets of eyes — the ones that remembered being high in a tree in the forest with Lotus on her lap, and the ones that had spent the last month zooming around on dragon back. Sapphire tried mostly to look through that second set of eyes. Even if Lotus didn't fly very high compared to most dragons, it was still off the ground.

They got this high all the time.

She sat, breathing in the new experience, letting it push out some of the old, stagnant fear. This wasn't so bad, even if she was clutching a tree trunk again, and with no dragon wings to help her land gently if she fell.

She snorted. Even when there *were* dragon wings available, the landings weren't generally all that gentle.

Carefully, she stood on the branch under her feet and stretched up. The tree branches were a lot thinner up here, and laden with apples that bent them down. Maybe they didn't have enough strength left to hold up an elf girl, even a light one. She moved one of her feet so her weight was spread over two branches, and felt a little steadier.

With her hands gripped tightly to the trunk, she tipped her head back and looked up. The top of the tree was still awfully far away. She was at least halfway up — maybe that was far enough.

She looked at one of the red apples hanging just above her shoulder. It looked ripe and tasty, just like the ones far over her head — and she could pick this one and be down the tree and enjoying the sunshine in less time than it took for Lotus to scarf down a bowl of milk curds.

Sapphire sighed and looked up again. This was just like jumping off the boulders. No one would have known if she'd eaten those apples with her feet firmly on the ground — but it would have felt like cheating.

She didn't want to feel like the girl who stopped halfway.

She wanted to feel brave.

Taking a deep breath, she reached for a branch just a little above her head. She didn't have to do this quickly. Her heart beat against her chest hard enough that she thought it might pop right out. She let it beat. Irin said it was okay to feel scared, so long as you kept doing your job.

Two more small steps up, and her palms were getting sweaty too. Sapphire rubbed them against her leggings, remembering the awful, cold, slick rain of two years ago. Every branch had been treacherous.

This wasn't that tree. This one was sun-warmed and old and bent from the weight of many seasons of apples hanging off its branches. The limbs under her hands were cool and strong and well used to creatures climbing them in search of crisp, sweet goodness. She let that soak into her skin and mix with the rain-drenched fear of two years ago.

One more small step up.

Sapphire reached up over her head for another handhold and realized there was nowhere left to go. She was at the top—up high enough that she could stretch her palm into the clear, bright sun.

Knowing it would be the hardest part, and wanting to get it over with, she looked down. Beyond her feet and beyond all the matte-gray branches and the leaf-cast shadows. To the ground, which still looked dizzyingly far away. Still made an elf girl of Moon Clan feel so very small and insignificant and helpless and scared. One slip and she would crack her head open, just like Lotus would do to the both of them if she caught an air current wrong or misjudged a distance or ran out of energy before she landed them both back safely on the ground.

Sapphire gulped. Irin was right—there was no way to do this brave stuff and not be scared. There were too many ways things could go wrong. Too many ways to fall out of an apple tree or off a dragon, or for a brave dragon like Kis to fall out of the sky and never fly again.

If she and Lotus wanted to fly high in the sky, they would have to know all that stuff and figure out how to be brave anyhow.

Sapphire could feel the shakes rising in her body. She held tight to the swaying branch that was all that was left of the apple tree's trunk up this high, pushed her face against its rough bark, and let the tears come. Two years' worth of them, running down her face in a waterfall of remembered terror and fear for herself and for the tiny creature who had loved her even then.

She had been so terribly scared, and so helpless — and that, maybe, was the worst of it.

She wasn't so helpless anymore. And neither was Lotus. They had learned how to be brave, and how to work together, and how to practice until they got something right.

Flying high was just one more lesson. One more thing to practice.

She wasn't a terrified elf girl high in a tree — not anymore. And Lotus wasn't a hatchling fresh out of an egg. Sapphire felt her tears trailing away as the big knot in her ribs untangled. She swiped at her cheeks, laughing as snot fell along with the tears. Hopefully it didn't land on any apples.

Then again, there were a couple of people who might deserve a snotty apple or two.

She grinned and swiped at her cheeks one more time. Then she reached up over her head, right up to the very top of the tallest tree in the orchard, and picked herself a red and juicy apple.

Chapter 18

Sapphire didn't know she was awake until she felt the hands shaking her.

Kellan was bent over her, eyes full of fear. "You were screaming this time. I'm going to get Karis."

"No need," said a voice from the door. "I'm already here." She walked into their rondo, Afran's huge eye peering through the door behind her.

Sapphire blinked — the big dragon rarely came this deep into the village.

A moment later, Lotus squeezed in and landed on Sapphire's bed in two quick hops. Her chirruping sounds were full of worry, and her claws had to be poking holes in the bed covers with how hard she was clutching.

"I'm okay." Sapphire tried to keep her very worried dragon from destroying everything in the small bedroom. "Hold still before you break the bed."

Lotus just chirruped louder — until Afran rumbled from the door.

"Indeed." Karis gave him a quick look. "This is no place for dragons, well behaved or otherwise." She gave Lotus a stern look and pointed at a spot on the floor by the bed. "Lie down there, and if I hear a peep out of you, I'm sending you back to Kis."

Sapphire stared as her dragon curled up on the floor, totally silent. "Wow — you have to teach me how to do that." Her voice sounded scratchy, and it hurt to talk.

Karis smiled. "Years of practice." She looked over at Afran. "This is mine to do, wise old man. Get everyone else settled, please, and I'll come to you when I can."

She waited while the large dragon backed himself slowly away from the door and began rumbling at whoever had gathered outside. From the sounds of it, half the village was out there. Kellan stood and took her cloak off a hook behind the door. "I'll go too. Maybe some hot tea will help everyone sleep."

Sapphire's head hurt — and for some reason, so

did her throat. She watched her best friend leave and then looked at Karis, who was sitting on the foot of her bed, idly scratching Lotus's tail with her foot.

The older woman studied her for a bit. "I'm sure Kellan will bring you some of that tea shortly. In the meantime, why don't you tell me why you woke up half the village with your screams?"

Sapphire's hand went to her throat. It felt raw inside. "I didn't know — I'm really sorry."

"You were sleeping." Karis's eyes were dark and serious. "I assume your dream wasn't a good one."

This one had been worse than all the others — but no one knew about any of those. Sapphire hung her head, ashamed and scared. "I've been having nightmares since I first arrived. I was hoping they would go away."

"Sometimes they do." The older woman sounded totally calm, like they were discussing what to put in the evening stew. "But when they don't, sometimes it can help to talk about it."

That required thinking about them. "I used to dream about being up in the big tree. Now I'm having nightmares about flying." That was as much as she intended to say on the subject.

"Ah." Karis was nodding, like that made total

sense. "And did they start when your flying lessons began?"

Sapphire looked down at the patched quilt on her bed and the three new holes from Lotus's claws. "Yes." She wanted to reach out and touch her dragon, but she remembered what Irin had said about passing on her fear. "This one was worse, though, and we didn't fly at all yesterday."

Karis was silent for a minute. "Did something else happen?"

Yes, Sapphire thought bitterly. She'd managed to climb an apple tree and feel a little bit brave. Which was clearly sheer foolishness. She and Lotus might not be a girl and a hatchling anymore, but they weren't big enough to take on raging winds and black maws and evil magics in the sky.

She wanted to curl up in a ball and cuddle up to Lotus and never sleep again.

Karis's hand reached out and stroked her hair. "Perhaps a bowl of soup, and then we'll talk of this more in the morning."

Bowls of soup didn't keep the dreams away — Sapphire knew that all too well. Nothing did.

Suddenly Lotus shot up from her neatly curled position by the bed and scurried out of the rondo, making wild chirruping sounds.

Karis watched her go, eyebrows high. "I wonder what's gotten into her?"

Sapphire had no idea, but she could hear running feet. Kellan came flying in the door, eyes wide. "Fendellen is coming!"

"Now?" Karis was on her feet, eyes almost as wide as the younger girl's. "It's the middle of the night."

"Afran says she bugled in his head and she'll be here any minute."

The older woman sprang into action. She gripped Kellan's shoulders tight enough to hold her still — mostly. "Go wake up Inga and get the kitchen going. Ask Afran to assemble an honor guard, quickly, and to send a message up to Elhen." She spun to Sapphire, hands moving almost as fast as her words. "You, go tell Lily and Alonia to wake people as quickly and quietly as they can — they'll deal better with a gentle wake-up at this hour of the night. Then go warn Irin that the nursery is about to get a little wild."

Sapphire was totally lost — this was more preparation than she'd ever seen for a visitor. "Who is Fendellen?"

Karis stopped in mid-motion and stared at her. "That's right — you weren't here the last time she came."

Kellan gulped. "Fendellen will be queen after Elhen passes to ashes. She's been out questing. No one has seen her for years."

Dragon royalty. Coming to visit, right now. Sapphire grabbed for her cloak, trying to remember all of Karis's rapid instructions. Irin first—Lily woke up cranky, and Alonia was impossible to wake up at all. They weren't going to get their eyes open until it was too late.

She pushed out the rondo door and ran into Kellan's back. Her best friend gasped and pointed to the sky.

Sapphire strained her eyes, looking. She couldn't hear or see anything.

And then she saw the dark, dragon-shaped shadow blotting out some of the stars. Lotus trembled beside her, and Sapphire reached out a hand, trying to stay calm. It was all too easy to remember the dream horror of falling from the sky.

This dragon wasn't falling, though. Even as just a shadow, she had the most graceful flight Sapphire had ever seen, as highly controlled as Afran but with more agile speed.

A *lot* more speed.

She held her breath as the shadow hurtled straight down at the bare patch in front of the rondo and executed a landing that didn't disturb a single mote of dust.

Sapphire stared at the elegant, shadowy lines of the new arrival and could barely breathe.

Karis stepped forward, hand over her heart. "Fendellen, I welcome you here on behalf of dragons and elves and humans all. We weren't expecting your visit, so we'll have a more appropriate welcome ready for you shortly."

"I would expect no less from Afran and his kin," said a clearly amused voice that sounded almost human. "But it's entirely unnecessary to get everyone out of bed at this hour."

"That will be for us to decide," said a gruff voice from the left. "I see you still like to make a dramatic entrance."

Sapphire gaped. Irin was speaking to the queen-to-be like she was one of his hatchlings.

"Irin." Fendellen's head maneuvered over to the big man and rubbed against his cheek. "How's Kis?"

"Cranky and stubborn and eating too much, same as always."

Fendellen's laugh rumbled hard enough to shake the ground. "Same as another old man I know."

Sapphire snorted and then slapped a hand

over her nose.

A bright dragon eye looked her direction. "You must be the girl who found a dragon egg in a tree. That was well done."

How did Fendellen know who she was? Somehow Sapphire managed to find her voice. "I didn't do so much. Mostly Lotus kept me warm, and then Karis and Afran helped get us down in the morning."

"It's a wise woman or dragon who knows when she needs help." Fendellen reached out her nose to Lotus, who had tried to hide herself behind a rain barrel. "You and your kin chose each other well, I think."

Lotus stayed mostly hidden, but the frenetic energy flowing down their bond quieted.

Irin harrumphed, stomping his feet against the cold. "I assume there's a good reason we're all standing out here in the middle of the night instead of greeting you in the morning like reasonable people."

Fendellen snorted smoke again. "Cranky old men are welcome to go to bed whenever they need to. I'm here to speak with Sapphire and Lotus."

Sapphire could scarcely believe her ears. "Why?"

"I see you in my dreams," said Fendellen quietly. "I see the two of you falling."

Embarrassment flooded Sapphire's cheeks. "I'm sorry."

"I'm not." The queen-to-be's voice was gentler now. "You are the first of the five who will save us, and that means your successes and your fears matter more than most. I've come to help." Fendellen raised her head, and this time her voice carried the ring of royalty. "I don't know why you must learn to fly high in the skies, young Sapphire and Lotus, but you must. It's entirely possible the future of dragonkind depends on it."

Sapphire could feel her knees shaking so hard, they were knocking together. "We've tried. We're not having much success."

"On the contrary. You've had good teachers and made excellent progress." Fendellen nodded at Karis and Irin in turn, and at a shadow that could only be Afran in the dark. Then she lowered her head to Kellan and winked. "You've even had the help of a most steadfast friend."

"Oh." A small, awed, yearning sound slid out of Kellan.

Sapphire had one moment of fierce, beating hope that a dragon was finally going to bond with her best friend — and then she saw the sadness in Fendellen's eyes.

The queen-to-be kept looking at Kellan. "You want, and you wait, and I don't know if you will ever have your heart's desire, child. But know that if it were up to me, I would find you entirely deserving."

Kellan's lips quivered, but she never looked away. "Thank you."

Fendellen snorted puffs out her nose. "I do, however, hear that you make an excellent meat pie. I would consider one of those a fine bribe in the morning if you'd like a ride out to the cliffs to watch the lesson."

Kellan's eyes widened as big as plates. "Yes. No. Yes. I'll be happy to make you meat pies. Dozens of them." She pulled up her cloak and bolted for the kitchen as fast as her feet could carry her.

Irin laughed. "Still eating like a hatchling, are you?"

The queen-in-waiting merely blew elegant puffs of smoke into the night sky.

Sapphire had so many questions. "What lesson?"

Fendellen looked at her again, and even in the dark, her eyes looked amused. "I'm the best flier of any dragon alive, my dear girl. If I can't get you into the high skies, no one can."

Sapphire could feel the skittering terror, and not all of it was hers. Lotus was panicking behind her rain barrel, hoping no one could see her.

"We'll go to the cliffs in the morning." Fendellen took a step toward Irin. "In the meantime, do you think Kis can be persuaded to move over enough to let me have a place to sleep?"

Sapphire knew that any dragon in the village would gladly give up their rondo for the night. Even Kis.

The tall, elegant dragon reached her nose down one last time and touched Lotus, still quivering behind the rain barrel. "Come, youngling. We'll go keep old Kis company while he snores, and I'll tell you about all the milk curds Irin burned when I was a baby."

Irin snorted. "You'd better tell her why I burned them."

Fendellen's laughter rang into the night—and stayed in Sapphire's ears long after she'd tucked herself back into bed.

Chapter 19

"Good morning."

The words, whispered in Sapphire's ear, nearly scared her to death—mostly because she hadn't realized she'd fallen back asleep again. She dragged an eye open and peered at Kellan, who looked far too cheerful in the dim light of dawn.

Memory flooded back. Kellan was cheerful because she was going to ride another dragon this morning—and because she'd probably been up all night baking meat pies. "Did you get any sleep?"

Kellan sat on the foot of the bed, a breakfast tray on her lap. "No. I was too excited. I brought you some breakfast."

Sapphire scowled at the bowl of oatmeal. That was definitely not meat pies. "I don't think I'm hungry."

"Inga said this will stick to your ribs, even if your fool dragon flies upside down and dumps you into the water."

The old woman who ruled the kitchen with an iron fist was never afraid to say the truth as she saw it, and this morning, that was oddly comforting. "That's probably a good reason to skip breakfast."

"No way. You know what Karis says about that, and she said she'd stop by to check on you in a bit."

Sapphire scowled and reached for the bowl on the tray. Karis would definitely make her eat it, and oatmeal went down way better while it was still warm. "I'm not an invalid."

"We know." Kellan glanced down at her knees, her voice quiet. "We're just feeling kind of strange because we've all tried to help you and Lotus fly, and the two of you have worked even harder, and now Fendellen's flown all the way back from the south oceans to help you. It's a big deal, but nobody wants to make you nervous by saying that. So we're going to make sure you eat breakfast instead."

The spoonful of oatmeal stuck in Sapphire's throat.

"She's an amazing flyer," Kellan said softly.

"If anyone can help, she can."

Too much of last night was streaming back into Sapphire's brain. "She has the dreams too. The ones where Lotus and I fall out of the sky. That can't be a good thing. Maybe we'll never learn, and something terrible will happen because we don't."

Kellan sat up straighter, eyes flashing. "Maybe the dreams are just the way she knew to come help you."

Maybe, but that wasn't the fear congealing in Sapphire's belly. "Maybe the Dragon Star picked the wrong elf." And maybe the wrong dragon, too, even though it felt horribly disloyal even to think it.

"At least you got picked."

Five quiet words — and they ripped Sapphire's heart right out of her chest. Kellan had waited her whole life for a dragon to choose her as kin. Worked longer and harder and done all the training and gotten all the bumps and bruises and sometimes, when she thought no one was listening, she cried herself to sleep at night and then got up in the morning and started working hard all over again.

Wishing and waiting for the same kind of bond that Sapphire had with Lotus.

Sapphire closed her eyes and let the magic of that bond flow through her. The love and the acceptance and a kind of deep, burbling joy that only happened when Lotus dreamed — or when she was trying to chase down a rabbit.

That kind of bond couldn't possibly be a mistake, and even if it was, Sapphire wasn't willing to let her dragon go. Which meant she didn't get to give up on either of them. She clenched her fists and tried to find some of the courage she'd felt at the top of the apple tree. "Maybe Fendellen will fly upside down with you today."

Kellan's cheeks turned a little white. "She's just giving me a ride to the cliff so I can watch."

Sapphire grinned. "I'll teach you the trick with your toes just in case." She held out her bowl. "Here, have some oatmeal. I hear it sticks to your ribs."

Kellan snorted. "You're not usually this mean."

Nothing about this day was usual. She was about to get a flying lesson — from a dragon who would one day be queen.

"Good. Somebody sent you a sensible breakfast." Karis took two steps in from the doorway and perched on the end of Kellan's bed. "Perhaps add a little cheese to that, or a handful of nuts."

Kellan jumped up. "I'll get both. And some

more cider." She paused halfway out the door. "Would you like something, Karis?"

"No, youngling, but thank you for asking."

Sapphire watched the back of her best friend disappear and gulped. Karis only came to student rooms if someone was sick or something very serious had happened. "Is Fendellen waiting?"

"Not yet. Irin says she and Lotus are both still sound asleep."

That was a minor miracle, given how jangly her dragon's brain had been after Fendellen's arrival. "That's a good thing, that she's sleeping." Sapphire gulped again and looked at Karis. "So she keeps her strength up for today."

"You don't have to worry about that." The older woman winked. "Do you know that Lotus is at her very strongest as a flyer right now? Her wings are as big as they're going to get, and her body's still small. One day, she'll have to work a lot harder at staying in the air, but right now, she's got everything she needs to keep the two of you aloft easily."

Sapphire thought about how big some of the dragons were. Afran's wings were much larger than Lotus's, but they were much smaller compared to his body — and Afran was a serene, elegant flyer who didn't ever look like he might fall out of the sky.

"That's why Fendellen's such a terror in the skies." Karis settled herself more comfortably, leaning her back against the wall and bending a foot up on her knee. "She's still young, and she has the biggest wingspan I've ever seen on a young dragon."

Maybe a story would help her breakfast go down. "It sounds like you know her pretty well."

"I do. Not as well as Irin and Kis, though." Karis chuckled. "She was the terror of the nursery before she became a terror in the skies. She made Kis roar more than all the other dragonets put together."

Sapphire had never heard Kis make a noise louder than a cranky rumble. "Was he fiercer back then?"

"He was angrier." Karis had a sad look in her eyes. "And I think he hurt less. The medicine Irin gives him now to keep the pain away makes him less irritable, but it also makes him sleepy. Back then, he was a bit of a menace, but the little ones loved him anyhow—dragon and elf and human all. They would gather round to listen to his stories, just like you do."

Sapphire blushed—she and Kellan often crept into the shadows of the nursery to hear Kis and Irin tell their tales, but she hadn't realized the adults of the village knew that. "It's a good time to visit. The stories help Lotus get to sleep." Her dragon's late-night antics were legendary. Kellan had learned to sleep through most of them, but Sapphire wasn't so lucky.

The price of being bonded with a small peach-pink terror.

Karis smiled. "When I'm out on tour, one of the things I miss most is the nursery tales." She reached out and ruffled Sapphire's hair. "I hear more noise outside, so it's time for me to be off and for you to get yourself ready for this morning's adventure."

That was one way to describe it. "They're probably placing bets on how long it will take for me to turn into an elf pancake." It had been one of the village's favorite amusements ever since their first flying lesson.

The older woman's lips twitched. "I think you'll find that most people are smart enough not to bet against a future queen."

Whoever did was going to make a killing. "Fendellen's not used to thinking about a rider."

"That's where you'd be wrong." Karis stood and smoothed the wrinkles in the blanket with her hand. "Dragon queens are born to rule, and that means they pay attention to anyone and anything that affects the dragons under their care. Fendellen has been readying for that responsibility since the day she hatched. She may not fly a rider herself, but she'll be as aware of your strengths and weaknesses as she is of her own."

"She should be," said a gruff voice from the door. "It took long enough to get that lesson through her thick skull."

Karis chuckled. "Spoken by a man who knows the exact thickness of his own." She ducked past a scowling Irin and paused in the doorway, looking back at Sapphire. "If it helps, Afran believes this just might work."

Irin watched her go, and then turned back, scowl still firmly in place. "I suppose everyone's been coming to fill you full of good wishes and encouragement."

He said the words like they tasted bad. Sapphire held up her bowl. "They've been filling me up with oatmeal, mostly."

That seemed to meet with his approval.

Which just made Sapphire crankier. "Did you come to deliver words of wisdom to the foolish elf before she falls off her dragon and plunges into the briny deep?" If she was going to end up the main character in a comic ballad, she might as well write a line or two for herself.

He snorted. "Feeling feisty this morning, are you? Good."

She hadn't been, but something about his gruff presence had shifted the energy in the small rondo. "Is someone feeding Lotus?" She could feel an awake presence on the other end of their bond.

Irin nodded. "Alonia and Lily are busy stuffing her full of milk curds."

That was good. Lotus liked milk curds a lot better than Sapphire liked oatmeal. She looked up at the stern man who had taught her more about perseverance than everyone else in the village combined. He hadn't come here to offer her words of encouragement — she knew that, but she wanted them anyhow. "Do you have any advice for me?"

He looked at her for a long moment. "Trust your bond. Trust your dragon. Know that the two of you together can do absolutely anything you need to do."

She could see it in his eyes — the shadows of the man and dragon who had made such a promise to each other before they hurtled into battle and almost certain death.

She'd always felt sorry for them both, so very sad for the old warrior and his cranky dragon with all his aches and pains. As she studied Irin, sitting there awkwardly on the edge of her bed, Sapphire realized the truth was something quite different. "You and Kis — you did that. You trusted your bond, and it made you something better.

Together."

He almost cracked a smile. "That we did."

She finished her thought because it was changing the way she would see the two of them forever. "And you still do that. Every day." She swallowed. "You're something better together than either of you could be alone."

He nodded very slowly — and it wasn't sadness she saw in his eyes. "Every day that Kis opens his eyes and I feel the bond is a victory." He reached for her hand. "Remember that, missy. There are worse things than falling out of the sky."

He swung her out of bed with a strength that belied his age. "And nothing better than soaring up into one. Go. Fendellen awaits you."

Chapter 20

The cliffs were so high, they were making Sapphire dizzy just looking down. Blue-green ocean waters spread out far below and all the way to the hazy horizon. She wished Kellan had stayed nearby, but her friend had hopped off, fed Fendellen half a dozen meat pies, and then gone off with Karis and Afran and several dozen others to a far-off perch of rocks.

An audience, but one wanting very much to stay out of the way.

"It's just the three of us." Fendellen's breath still smelled vaguely of meat pies. "Let those on the rocks give you fortitude and hope because what you do this morning is for them as much as it is for you. And then forget they are there. It's just the three of us and a beautiful open sky calling our names."

Sapphire closed her eyes and tried not to whimper. Death felt imminent, and everyone, from her best friend to her new flying instructor, was far too cheerful. Lotus quivered at her side and ducked her head behind Sapphire's back.

Sapphire gulped. Lotus hadn't even been able to look over the cliff's edge.

If the queen-to-be could sense their fear, she gave no sign of it. Fendellen gestured at the group on the far-off rocks. "They've taught you well, each from what they know. You've learned efficient competence from Karis, elegant precision from Afran, stubborn diligence from Irin, and joy from your young friend so recently on my back."

Those sounded exactly right, and yet somehow they hadn't been enough.

"I am here to teach you something that only one who will be queen can know." The ice-blue dragon stretched out her wings in the cool morning sun. "There is much that rides on the two of you. You are marked by the Dragon Star, and the very existence of dragonkind might well rest on your shoulders."

Sapphire tried to choke back the rising tears. She didn't feel remotely capable of being that important.

"The reasons you need to do this are vast and important, and so much depends on your bravery and your choices." Fendellen's nose dropped right in front of Sapphire's face, so close she could feel the dragon's hot breath on her cheeks. "I'm here to tell you that if you think about all that, you'll never get off this cliff."

Sapphire stared.

Fendellen puffed amused smoke. "I'm not Irin, youngling. He'll have made sure that your very important reasons for not quitting are part of the fabric of who you are — and if you ever want to give up, I'll be right behind him in line to remind you why you can't. But until that moment comes, you need to be a girl and her dragon. Nothing more, nothing less."

Sapphire's insides felt all topsy-turvy. "Isn't that what we've been doing?"

"Yes." Blue eyes twinkled. "But you believe you're a girl and her dragon who can't fly. That's the part we need to change."

The urge to stomp her feet and kick the cliff to smithereens was huge. "I've. Tried." Sapphire got the words out through gritted teeth.

"Yes, you have. But you're trying to do it with an act of your will. You hope that if you can wrap your fears up tightly enough, you might be able to do this."

It was either that or let them eat her whole.

::No.:: Fendellen shook her head, her mind voice exceedingly gentle. ::Your battle is not with the fear, young kin. You need to make space for something else to rise up inside you instead.::

Sapphire felt at least as cranky as Kis on a very bad day. "Like what?"

::Watch. Listen. Feel.:: The queen-to-be flapped her wings once and sailed off the edge of the cliff.

Sapphire shivered as the sensation of flight touched her mind. Somehow, Fendellen was keeping a channel open.

::I am,:: came the wry reply. ::It's not all that easy without a kin bond, so I'd appreciate it if you paid close attention. What do you feel?::

The sensation of lightness, of lifting. "You like this." Sapphire spoke out loud and trusted that the ice-blue dragon would hear her somehow. "It's a bit like when Lotus does her barrel rolls."

::Yes. She's a dragon. We're born for this. This is where we find our greatest joy.:: Fendellen swooped down, riding a current, and then blazed a trail high into the sky.

Sapphire followed with her eyes, but it was the feelings that exploded in her mind that had her awestruck. Wild, blazing happiness. A dragon laying down her burdens and the weight of who she would one day need to be and rising, weightless, into the early morning sky.

::You see more than I thought you might.::

It was impossible to miss. "You get to be free up there."

No more thoughts came down the mind bond. Only wordless invitation.

Sapphire looked at the peach-pink creature beside her, small dragon body hunched over in fear. For some reason, Fendellen had not chosen to share this with Lotus.

::Indeed.:: A shadow spiraled above them, coming closer. ::That is for you to do, young Sapphire. She will find it far easier to believe coming from you than from me.::

That didn't seem possible. "You will be her queen."

::Yes.:: Fendellen wasn't far above their heads now. ::But you're the one she loves, and the one she fears she will fail.::

Sapphire reached out to scratch the head of the dragon she loved more than anything or anyone, and knew every word of the queen-in-waiting's message to be true. Which meant her job wasn't to hide her fear at all. It was to beam her love and trust into every scale of a scared dragon's soul.

The darkness that had been stalking Sapphire for weeks fled. It wouldn't serve them now. It was time to be the light. She reached for Lotus and cupped a peach-pink head in her hands and let excitement shine in her eyes. "Let's go have some fun."

Their bond lurched, confused, and Lotus chirruped in the whirring way of a tiny hatchling.

They weren't tiny anymore. Sapphire grinned. "Cliffs are just big boulders. We've totally got this."

Green dragon eyes looked at her suspiciously.

Fendellen was right — this was all about trust, and she totally hadn't been doing her job. "I bet a barrel roll out over the water feels really cool." And if she fell off, at least they would know where to look for her body.

But she wasn't going to fall off. They were done with that. Babies fell over learning to walk all the time, but they got up again and kept trying and one day, they didn't fall on every third step anymore. It was time to believe they weren't babies. She had a good spot to tuck her feet, an apple in her pocket, and a dragon who knew how to do exuberant joy better than anyone.

It was time to do it high up in the sky.

Sapphire swung a leg over Lotus's back and

tucked her feet under wings that were beginning to unfurl. And then she looked up at Fendellen, hovering in a tight circle over their heads, and laughed. "Race you to the edge of the sky."

The ice-blue dragon blasted an amused trumpet, flapped her mighty wings, and streaked off.

The body under Sapphire's legs snapped into action, and Lotus hurled herself off the cliff, entirely intent on chasing the streak in the distance. Sapphire squealed as a tunnel of air nearly knocked her off, and tucked her body down tight against her dragon's neck.

Water sped by underneath them, a blue-green blur dusted with specks of white. The air grabbing at Sapphire's leggings was cool and damp, and somewhere off in the distance, she could hear the cheering of the crowd on the rocks. Watching them fly.

Watching them *fly*.

The speck ahead of them trumpeted again. With approval this time. With pride, and with loud, royal challenge. Fendellen flipped over and executed a very nifty barrel roll.

Wild glee gusted through the kin bond, and Sapphire had no idea which end it started from.

Lotus stretched her wings higher, harder,

faster, everything in her intent on catching that growing dragon-shaped speck. Sapphire put more weight into her feet and let herself be as light as a cloud, as sticky as a stinkberry burr. She kept one hand wrapped fiercely around Lotus's neck spines, but with the other one, she reached into her pocket, pulled out the apple, and took the biggest bite she could manage.

Love. Trust. In the two who flew as one.

Lotus found some other gear and shot forward into the light.

They totally had this.

Chapter 21

Sapphire had no idea how long it took them to catch Fendellen, or how long the bigger dragon danced alongside Lotus's maiden flight in the morning sky.

She only knew that they drank deeply of freedom, of lightness, of a joy that grew them into a shape that could never go back to what they'd been before, and when there was not a drop of energy left in either of them, they landed on a sunny spot on the cliffs. Lotus fell over where she landed, panting and looking like the happiest dragon in this world or any other one.

Sapphire kept her act together long enough to offer her exhausted dragon some of the water they'd left on the cliff, and even a few milk curds. And then she dropped to the rock, leaned her back against Lotus's warm belly, and let herself breathe in the wonder of what they'd done.

She felt, more than heard, Fendellen settling on the rock beside them. The queen-to-be had taken one last solo circle in the morning sky.

Sapphire tried to hold up an arm and discovered they weren't working any longer. "I have some milk curds if you want them."

The dragon's rumble sounded oddly like Irin's chuckle. "I think you'll have need of those when your young dragon wakes up."

A remnant bubble of wild joy found its way loose and rose up long enough to keep Sapphire's eyes open. "We did it."

"You did." Fendellen nodded, eyes regal and proud. "There is something inside Lotus that needs to fly to be whole, just as you needed a dragon to be whole. Today, you have given her that gift. Only her kin could have done that. Today, you've fully honored all of who you are."

Sapphire swallowed. That was high praise for what had basically been a game of tag in the sky. "Thank you."

"Your path ahead will not always be easy," the elegant dragon said quietly. "So remember this day, young Sapphire. One day the dragons will need you, and this joy is part of what will carry you

242

through."

They were one of the five who would save dragonkind. Sapphire knew she couldn't hide that away any longer, any more than she could hide her fear. A lesson she had just been taught by someone who must understand it very well. She tilted her head and looked up into wise eyes that were still so very young. "Your path must not be very easy either."

Fendellen bobbed her head. "There will be hard days for me too." She leaned down to Lotus, who was sound asleep on the sunny rock where she'd landed, and nuzzled the small dragon's cheek. "Just remember that two together are stronger, always."

Sapphire picked up a flicker of loneliness, and she realized it was coming from the ice-blue dragon. The one who had chosen no kin. "I have three friends who aren't bonded yet." She wanted to be fair to all of them, but her heart cried out to add the next words. "Kellan has waited so long."

Fendellen looked sad for a moment. "She isn't meant to be mine, although I wish it were so. Her heart is as big as any I've ever met."

Queens sometimes saw things — maybe queens-in-waiting did too. "Do you know if she will have a dragon?"

Another flicker of sadness, and the ice-blue

dragon turned her gaze out over the waters. "I don't know."

Sapphire didn't ask anything else, but she had the oddest sensation that the answer hadn't been the truth.

Fendellen turned back, and the sadness was gone from her eyes. "What I do know is that when you flew off the cliff, it was Kellan who pushed hardest. You'll want to thank her for that."

Sapphire squinted her eyes, her tired body and even more tired brain not understanding. "What do you mean?"

Fendellen puffed smoke in a way that spoke of amusement. "I borrowed Lovissa's trick. The mind bond, the one that let you feel the pleasure of my flight—Afran and Kis helped hold that, and they pulled in their kin and a few others. The ones who love you best."

She hadn't jumped alone. Somehow she had known that, but it settled something deep in her heart to have it confirmed. "I bet Karis was pushing too. And Irin just grumped and tossed me an apple."

"No." Fendellen shook her head slowly. "Karis believed you would fly without anyone needing to push. Irin..." She paused, and the sadness in her eyes was a deep, fathomless pool. "He was working very hard to keep Kis on the ground."

Tears flooded Sapphire's eyes. "Kis was here? On the cliffs?"

The ice-blue dragon nodded slowly. "Yes. He loves Lotus. There was no one prouder when she flew."

Sapphire thought of all the nights her small dragon had curled up next to the cranky old warrior and gone to sleep. "She loves him right back."

"He knows that." Fendellen's eyes turned toward the far rocks. "And with the mind bond wide open, I was able to send them back your joy. Mostly to Kis. He needed it most."

There was something in the queen-to-be's voice that caught at Sapphire's heart. "You were a hatchling. In the nursery with Kis."

"Yes." A long pause as a dragon remembered. "I love him too. Very much. Because he tried to give his life to save those I will one day rule — and because he cuddled a cheeky dragonet close and sang her grumpy lullabies even when she tried to set him on fire."

Sapphire breathed in. One day, she might have to do something big to save dragonkind — but she would be flying in the footsteps of greatness and learning from the very best.

That was something she could hold onto with both hands — or none at all.

"I must go now." Fendellen turned away from the cliff's edge. "Practice often, you two."

So that one day they would be ready.

The ice-blue dragon whiffed softly and then lifted up into the morning sky. ::Yes. And so that in the meantime, you will know joy.::

She turned her gaze on a sleeping Lotus. ::I will see you in the skies.::

38519757R00148

Made in the USA
Middletown, DE
20 December 2016